THE JUBILEE LETTER

The letter had been lost in the post for fifty years. But for Avril it solved a mystery, which had unsettled her since the Queen's Coronation — when she was young and in love . . . There had been two suitors to choose from: was Avril tempted by charming Jack or quiet Gordon? Both Jack and Gordon had secrets, and it was only when Avril discovered what they were hiding that she had been able to choose a love to last a lifetime.

CAROL MACLEAN

THE JUBILEE LETTER

Complete and Unabridged

LINFORD
Leicester

First published in Great Britain in 2012

First Linford Edition
published 2013

*A catalogue record for this book is available
from the British Library.*

ISBN 978–1–4448–1613–6

Published by
F. A. Thorpe (Publishing)
Anstey, Leicestershire

Set by Words & Graphics Ltd.
Anstey, Leicestershire
Printed and bound in Great Britain by
T. J. International Ltd., Padstow, Cornwall

This book is printed on acid-free paper

1

The letter arrived just as Avril was settling down to watch the start of the Queen's Diamond Jubilee celebrations. John and Lisa had bought a giant flat-screen television especially for the occasion, and late the previous evening it had been ceremoniously lifted and attached to the living-room wall.

Avril had pretended not to hear her eldest son's muted swearing as he tried to connect a snake of cables to the monster, accompanied by helpful suggestions from her grandson Alexander. Jennifer, Alex's wife, bouncing the new baby on her hip, gave Avril a conspiratorial smile.

Looking at the baby gave Avril a strange pang, right there in her chest where her heart lay. It was so strong a sensation that it felt like a physical pain, acid and yet sugar-sweet all at the same time.

She was a great-grandmother twice over, what with the new baby and her darling Lucy, the baby's four-year-old sister. When she felt that pang it was as if layers and layers of days rose, fluttering towards her like delicate chiffon. They peeled away and she felt anew the shock and surprise of being an old lady of eighty. Which was silly, wasn't it, for her bones could have told her that. Indeed they sang to her every morning as she creaked out of bed.

'GiGi! GiGi! Look,' Lucy shouted, waving her little hands high above her head.

GiGi was Lucy's special name for Avril. 'Great Grandmother' and even 'Great Gran' having proved too much for her to get her tongue around, Lucy had come up with the letter 'G' twice, the way she was taught to sound it at pre-school. Guh Guh. Soon it had mutated to GiGi. It was a secret message of love between them and only

Lucy was allowed to use the name. It remained to be seen whether baby brother Ross would be granted permission in due course or not.

'What is it, darling?' Avril asked. She fumbled for her glasses and balanced them on her nose.

'I'm on the telly,' Lucy yelled with glee.

And sure enough, she was! Avril blinked in amazement. It wasn't actually Lucy, but a cartoon likeness which bent and waved and jumped just when the real Lucy did.

'It's just the Xbox Kinect, Gran.' Inge, aged twelve, flopped heavily onto the sofa beside her. Her lips were sulky with attitude and she chewed and blew gum bubbles with a series of loud snapping sounds.

Avril patted her grand-daughter's hand, noticing how smooth Inge's skin was compared to the gnarled furrows and ridges of her own flesh.

'It's like magic to me, love. When I was your age . . . '

Avril trailed off. Young people didn't want to hear about the distant past. It bored them. It was black and white; sepia or Technicolor at best. Whereas Inge's world was full of bright colours, vibrant with the latest fashions and the must-have digital technology.

But Inge's hand curled gently around hers with affection and love. Even if it wasn't 'cool' to hang out with your Gran.

'I know — when you were my age you were either down a mine or up a chimney.'

'Not quite,' Avril protested. 'Those days were long gone by the time I was born, you know.' Then she noticed Inge's grin. 'You are naughty,' she scolded, smiling.

There was a sudden rattle of German behind them. Petra, Inge's older sister, was leaning over the back of the sofa. It was funny how life turned out, Avril mused. They'd fought the Germans tooth and nail. She'd been a child growing up in the war years, and her

4

father had almost lost his life to a German bullet. They had all suffered, all been marked in some way by those terrible years and their aftermath. Then her youngest son, Graham, ended up working and living in Southern Germany and marrying a German girl called Hildegard. Their daughters, Petra and Inge were being brought up there and were bilingual.

Avril had come to terms with it very quickly, was extremely fond of Hildegard and loved her grand-daughters. But she wondered what her father would have made of it. He was probably spinning in his grave right now, hearing Petra speak her mother tongue. As for Avril's mother, she would likely not have let them in the house.

Avril drifted into the layers of chiffon. She could see her mum clearly if she focused. There she was, standing ramrod straight at the front of her boarding house, mop in hand. She was wearing her usual spotless housecoat

5

and her hair was neatly tied and covered by a flowered scarf. She was frowning at Avril, disapproving of the company she was keeping, a deep vertical line carved between her dark brows from habit.

'Gran!' Petra was shaking her shoulder. 'Look! There's a letter for you.'

'A letter? But how did it find me here?' Avril was confused. It happened more and more often these days. Things she should know with the snap of her fingers were unfathomable.

'It didn't come in the post here.' Petra shook her head impatiently. 'Mum went to your house to water the plants and feed the cats, remember? She picked up your mail for you.'

Ah, yes, she did remember Hildegard's kind offer. John and Lisa were hosting the family party over a few days, and they were ensconced in their guest bedroom. It meant their own house was empty over this special Diamond Jubilee holiday.

Graham arrived, bringing the warm,

early summer air with him. He kissed Avril's papery cheek. 'Hello, Mum. Inge looking after you okay?' He ruffled his daughter's glossy blonde hair and she snapped her gum at him, annoyed.

'It's a full house, isn't it? I don't know how Lisa's managed to fit us all in,' Graham continued. 'Still, the kids will be fine in sleeping bags on the floor. Alex and Jennifer and the wee ones have a bedroom upstairs. What a shame Mark can't make it.'

Mark was Avril's middle son. He'd never married and lived a wandering life, following his career path around the globe.

'Where is he now again?' Avril asked. 'Remind me, darling.'

'I think it's Bolivia. No hang on, that contract was up last month, so it's Russia now.'

'Georgia,' John corrected, shouting through from the hall and appearing rather ruddy and flushed from the heat. 'Honestly, gathering this family for a celebration is like herding cats. Where's Dad?'

'He's having a nap but he'll be down in time,' Avril soothed, a lifetime of experience coming into play as she calmed her highly strung eldest child.

'We don't want to miss the processions,' John said worriedly. 'Nor the pageant of boats on the Thames.'

'And all the parties around the country,' Lisa added, joining them with a vast tray of snacks and drinks. 'That's the best bit for me. I love seeing the ordinary people enjoying themselves and taking part in such a wonderful and important royal occasion. It's history in the making, isn't it? We all want to be a part of it and to be there on this special day.'

'Are we having a party?' Lucy clapped her hands excitedly.

'Oh, yes, is there going to be a street party?' Avril asked. 'Do you know, I remember the street party we held for the Queen's Coronation in 1953. It was wonderful. I can still see the glorious piles of food and the beautiful illuminations. Oh, and the dancing. I did love to dance.'

She felt herself disappearing again into the gauzy past, only to be brought back by John's embarrassed voice.

'Sorry folks, there'll be no street party. For a start, we don't know any of our neighbours.'

Not to know their neighbours! How was it possible, Avril thought, to live in a street for twenty years the way John and Lisa had done, and not be familiar with the people who lived nearby? Life had changed drastically since her own youth. She could remember all the families who had lived in Aline Street, Glasgow, alongside their boarding house.

Yet, when she thought of where she lived now in a small modern bungalow in a quiet cul-de-sac, she had to agree with John. She knew only a handful of the neighbours. They were all so busy at work or otherwise away. She could tag them mainly by the cars they drove.

'And it's not the sort of place for street parties,' John added apologetically, indicating outside the window. They lived in a well-off suburb of the city where large stone houses were set discreetly back from the road, sheltering behind thick shrubberies and muted fencing.

'What a shame. Well never mind, we'll have our own party,' Avril said brightly. 'Let's get the telly on, see what's happening.'

There was a minor hubbub as Lucy was pulled kicking from the Xbox Kinect and the television images sought and found. Then there was the question of where everybody would sit. That, at least, was one of the advantages of age, Avril thought. She had a comfortable seat on the sofa and no argument about it. The younger people ran about as if playing musical chairs, and then were tipped off by their parents anyway to end up sprawled on beanbags on the carpet.

Lisa patiently ferried in pots of tea

and a large cafetière of coffee, while Hildegard cut cake and Lucy pretended to share out the crisps while managing to cram as many as possible into her own mouth.

The Queen appeared on the screen, looking serene and happy on this momentous occasion. There was a round of shushing in the family as everyone strained to hear the commentary.

'You forgot about your letter, Gran,' Petra whispered and tucked it into Avril's cardigan pocket, thinking perhaps that she would keep it for later, after the ceremonies.

Avril watched the figures on the screen. The live feed cut to old black and white footage of the Queen's Coronation, and the line between past and present blurred and wavered. She remembered watching the Coronation as it happened, and the sheer excitement of seeing it on their brand new television that Mum and Dad had bought specially for the event. The neighbours had squeezed in too, watching eagerly, until there was standing room only.

'Am I late?' the man asked and Avril, hearing that dear voice, felt her heart pound a little faster in anticipation of his nearness. But she wasn't sure whether she was hearing it here and now, or in the boarding house front room, squeezed in as she was between Gloria and Shirley, with Mr Manderley the butcher standing in front of them and partially obscuring their view with his round head and sticking-out ears.

In her pocket she felt the sharp edges of the envelope and heard the rustle of its crinkled paper. Puzzled, she slipped her fingers into her pocket and drew it out.

The envelope was wrinkled and watermarked as though it had lain somewhere damp for quite a while. The address was written in a neat, inked hand in the old style. It was all loops and curls carefully formed as if with great concentration. The original address thus beautifully wrought, had been scored through twice and two other addresses scribbled hastily on top. The letter had been following her, it seemed, from house to house, but at one point it had stopped on its journey and waited.

For what? Avril wondered hazily.

'That's a funny stamp,' Jennifer remarked from her seat beside her. 'Do you mind if I have a look?'

Avril allowed Jennifer to take the envelope from her hands and watched her stare at it.

'That's strange — look at the post-mark and the date,' Jennifer exclaimed. 'I can't believe it. Look, Alex, does that date really say 1962? That's impossible, surely.'

Then they were all crowding round, adding to the clamour from the television music. Avril let them pass it around. She looked for him as she waited. There he was, her darling husband, in the big, old armchair in the corner. He winked at her. *Am I late?* So

13

she hadn't heard it at the Coronation party. No, that's right, they were here, watching the Diamond Jubilee.

'It's not impossible, 'Alex was saying, shaking his head knowledgably. 'I've heard of such things happening before, letters getting lost in the post and arriving years later. Let's see, this was sent to Granny in 1962, so . . . ' He screwed up his eyes to mentally calculate. 'It's arrived fifty years late. Wow!'

'The local press would love a story like this,' Jennifer announced, holding the envelope as if it were an ancient and rare artefact. 'We should contact them.' She was a journalist by training and knew a good story when she saw one.

'We should let Mum decide about that,' John said firmly, taking the envelope from his daughter-in-law's grasp and returning it to Avril.

At that moment the TV camera zoomed in on the royal princesses' outfits and the family's attention fixed again on the bright screen.

But not Avril. Slowly she turned the envelope over and slid a fingernail under the gummed edge. The gum was brittle and gave easily. Inside was a single sheet of paper.

Had she somehow evoked this letter, caught as she was today between present and past? The chiffon layers wafted towards her, clinging to her hair and wrapping themselves baby-soft around her face.

Avril turned the letter over and began to read. There was a hollow ringing in her ears. And the past, never far away, swept her up and carried her rushing like a river, down the years and the months and the days.

2

Luscious. Luscious what? Strawberries, maybe? It was a good word. It rolled around satisfyingly in her mouth, full and fat and interesting. Avril lay on her stomach on her bed, with her legs bent up behind her to the air. They kicked rhythmically as she pondered. In front of her lay open a lined notebook and into this she scribbled ideas, nibbling on the end of her pencil in between thoughts.

'Avril? Avril!' Her mother's piercing call up the stairs shattered her train of thought. 'Have you finished cleaning that room? The new lodger will arrive after lunch.'

Avril sighed and shut her notebook. She rolled over onto her back and suppressed the urge to scream.

'Avril!' Her mother's tread could be heard on the staircase and her tone was severe.

Avril sat up, but it was too late. Linda Garnett stood framed in the doorway, frowning furiously at her elder daughter.

'What on earth are you doing, lying down in the middle of the day? Are you ill?'

'No, I was just . . . '

'Oh, I see now what you were doing, missy. Daydreaming as usual, wasting your time. Wasting *my* time. If you don't clean that room, who's going to have to do it? That's right, me. As if I don't have enough to do, what with Mrs Petrocelli's special diet and Mr Phillips's little problem.'

'We do have a National Health Service now. Maybe Mr Phillips should speak to his doctor and get some help,' Avril suggested, trying to deflect the rest of the conversation which she knew was coming.

'Mr Phillips won't go near a doctor or a hospital. It's his firm belief that if he goes to hospital he'll come out dead.' Linda Garnett shuddered. 'And I can't say I blame him. For all their new-fangled ideas for the nation's health, the hospital is still a grim place.'

She stopped and looked at Avril, the habitual deep groove in her forehead easing a little. 'Now, love, I do need you to finish that room. It's hard on you, I know, helping me out running the boarding house but goodness knows I couldn't do it without you. It's not as if your father's any help.'

She patted Avril's knee. 'Besides, you're twenty-one. It won't be too long before some handsome young man whisks you off your feet and into a decent marriage. Then you'll be set — you won't have to work any more. You can keep a tidy house for your husband and be a good mother and bring up your family.'

'What if I don't want to do that? What if I want to . . . ' *To write and sell my pieces?* Avril smoothed her skirt down, and tried again. 'Remember Annie Smith from school? She's working as a secretary in a big firm in London.'

Linda looked scandalised. 'Well, that's all very well for her. I won't see my daughter living like that. Imagine, a single girl living away from her parents, out until all hours and hobnobbing with goodness knows who. It's unseemly, that's what it is. It's dangerous, too. A girl can get a reputation if she's not careful.'

Her mother was right, Avril knew that. But there was a restlessness to her that she couldn't extinguish. A need for something . . . something more to life than living here at the old boarding house, followed by marriage to some dull man and endless years of more and more of the same sort of days.

There was a well of ideas and imagination within her that simmered and bubbled and sometimes threatened to explode like a volcano. She wrote as an outlet for it, letting her frustration spill over onto the clean white pages in the form of words and sketches. If her mother only knew what she'd done with a few of her outpourings, she'd be horrified.

Avril hugged her secret to herself, letting it warm her through the monotony of the days. It was a tiny ray of hope, and it was hers alone.

'So did you do it?' Linda was asking sharply.

Avril jumped as if her mother had cut decisively right into her mind and had seen what she had done. With relief, Avril realised she was talking about the room. Old Mr Grimshaw had left to live with his widowed sister in Yorkshire last week, and her mother had been pleased to get another lodger so quickly and at such short notice. Avril had seen the letter. A Mr Gordon Silver was to arrive that afternoon by train from Inverness.

She could see him in her mind's eye already. Most likely another crusty old gentleman with the standard bushy white moustache and whiskery cheeks, wearing a mustard check jacket and smelling faintly of damp and dogs.

Still, Mr Grimshaw had been a good

lodger, always paying his rent on time and keeping himself to himself with no noise. She wouldn't miss his false teeth, though. He set them beside his plate at dinner and Avril couldn't help being mesmerised by them as she served up the food.

'Yes, Mum, I did clean the room. It's all ready.'

'You're a good girl, Avril Garnett. Now do me a favour and take your Dad his lunch, will you? It's in the kitchen, wrapped up in a napkin.'

Linda kissed the top of her daughter's head and then Avril heard the clatter of her heels down the stairs, followed by the clank of the metal pail and then the slap slosh of the wet mop.

Bing Crosby crooned to her mother from the radio and Avril heard her joining in. Bing was her mother's favourite and she knew all the words to his songs. It was the only time when her mother seemed happy, singing along to the radio as she cleaned and cooked. It always reassured Avril that all was well after all.

She tucked her notebook out of sight under her pillow and stepped out onto the top landing. The boarding house was large and threadbare. The carpets were scalped in places down to the linen mesh holding the fibres together. The big, old sash windows rattled in the slightest of breezes and let in all manner of chill, damp air.

There were seven bedrooms in all, six upstairs and one down. Downstairs too, there was a kitchen, bathroom, living room and dining room. Avril liked to imagine the house in its heyday, with rich Tobacco Lords living in it. There would be luscious, thick Turkish carpets, swish velvet drapes covering the windows and, of course, plenty of food every mealtime — and none of it would have potatoes!

Along the corridor, competing with Bing Crosby, came the treacle sounds of Nat King Cole. There was a pause while the gramophone was brought screechily to a halt. Then a voice singing lustily in imitation of what had just gone before. It wasn't too bad an impersonation, although her brother's voice was thinner and less gritty than the King's. She pushed open his bedroom door and peeked in.

'Hey, Avril, listen to this and tell me if it's okay,' Davey said, grinning. He was older than her by two years and unlike most big brothers, he was good fun and nice to her. He spent most of his free time with his guitar and gramophone records, trying to sing like his heroes. She suspected he hummed his way through his work as a clerk at the shipyards too.

'I'll listen,' she agreed. 'But it'll have to be quick. I've got to go and take Dad his lunch. Unless you want to do that?' she finished hopefully.

He shook his head, then bent it down to his guitar, already absorbed in its twanging chords. The exposed back of his neck was curiously vulnerable and made her want to cry. She was soft. She welled up at anything, like cruelty to animals or a sad film. Her mother was forever telling her to toughen up.

Her Dad would wink, though. He'd defend her, telling her mother to leave her alone, she was doing all right.

That reminded her, he would most definitely be looking for his lunch by now. She waved hastily to Davey and turned, only to be almost floored by Gloria and Shirley running along the landing at her.

'Ouch,' Avril yelped, stroking her stomach tenderly where Gloria's sharp elbow had connected in her haste to get to her.

'Sorry.' Gloria laughed, unrepentant, brandishing a magazine in her face.

'You've got to see this,' gushed Shirley, a mirror image of her twin, with curly brown hair and bright blue eyes that looked like sunshine on the sea.

The twins laid out the magazine on the landing floor and pulled Avril down to hunker around it. Shirley pulled a bag of nougat from her pocket and offered it to Avril. Since sweet rationing had stopped two months before, all the kids had gone crazy buying toffee apples, licorice strips and lollipops. The twins were never without a paper bag of sweets.

'Isn't that gorgeous?' Gloria sighed and pointed.

Avril looked. It was an advertisement for children's denims and showed two rosy-cheeked girls wearing denim trousers and open-necked check shirts.

'Do you think Mum would let us get some trousers?' Shirley asked plaintively.

Avril knew exactly what her mother's response would be. *Over my dead body*. She could hear it now.

Too kind-hearted to tell them, she said only, 'I suppose you could ask. But I'd wait a bit, Mum's really busy today.'

She left them arguing about it and went downstairs to the kitchen to pick up her father's lunch.

★   ★   ★

The allotments were a five-minute walk from Aline Street. They took up most of what had been a formal park before the war. It had all been dug up and planted with potatoes and carrots as part of the war effort, and never reverted back to flowers. The fact was that people still needed to supplement their bought food with home-grown veg. But she would have liked to see flowers.

Avril gave the chickens a wide berth. They were irritable birds with sharp, pecking beaks and no fear of humans. There was her father's wooden shed, the door ajar and the telltale rope of blue smoke wafting from it. As she approached, she heard him cough, a deep chesty rattling that went on and on.

'You shouldn't smoke that,' she said sternly, handing over the wrapped sandwiches.

'It does me good,' her father said, slipping the pipe onto the shelf beside him. 'Thanks for these. Fancy one?'

26

They munched together contentedly on cheese and pickles.

'So how's the veg doing, then?' Avril asked dubiously. There was little sign of any greenery on the neatly raked soil beds.

David Garnett pulled himself up shakily from his battered chair. A German bullet had sliced through him in North Africa, nicking his spine and taking a neat chunk of his torso with its exit. He was lucky to be able to walk. He never spoke of his experiences in the war, and the family had learned not to ask.

So Avril suppressed her desire to leap up and help him. She waited while he slowly made his way out of the shed, to stand wheezily at the edge of the tilled earth.

'Damn chickens,' he puffed, then winked at Avril. 'I can blame them for lack of results, see. Anyway it's only the end of April and I started late. The plants'll be shooting up soon enough, you'll see.'

'At least eggs are off rations now,' Avril commented. 'So you won't need to bend to find the eggs here.'

'Ah, but bought ones don't have the same taste, lass,' her father said. Another fit of coughing sent him back to his seat in the shed. He wiped his mouth carefully with his red handkerchief. Then he picked up his pipe and the tin of tobacco and began to pack the bowl with spicy wads of the stuff. It was such a familiar scent. It would forever mean Dad and his allotment when she smelled it.

Avril's eyes glistened. She was soft, just as Mum accused her of being!

'Has Gordon arrived yet?' David asked, taking a great suck of the pipe stem and puckering out fat puffs of fragrant smoke.

'Gordon? Do you mean the new lodger? I didn't know that you knew him.' Avril was surprised — her mother hadn't mentioned it.

'He's a good lad. Remember that, not judging a book by its cover, as your

28

Granny would have said,' her father muttered enigmatically.

Avril didn't puzzle on what he meant because she'd only heard one word.

'Lad? You mean he isn't an ancient man like Mr Grimshaw?' Maybe the new lodger would turn out to be more interesting than she'd thought.

'Not ancient, no. Gordon must be about, what, twenty-six or twenty-seven. His father was my best friend. We fought together during the war. Looked out for each other's backs.'

David Garnett was silent, his eyes to the hedge at the end of the allotment but seeing across a foreign ocean and across the years to scenes which Avril could not share.

'You didn't tell me you had a best friend,' she answered softly, hoping that he would say more. She'd never heard him share so much, ever. When she mulled it over, her father had appeared to have no friends at all.

There was Bert, of course, who had the adjacent allotment plot and he played cards with Mr Phillips. There was her mother, too, but that was different. They couldn't very well be called 'friends', could they? Her mother spent all her time trying to get her father out from under her feet. Which was probably why he so often retired here to his shed for peace.

'Dad?' Avril prompted.

'He was killed in the campaign in North Africa. The blast knocked him back into me. He died in my arms,' David announced bluntly.

Avril reached impulsively to hug him but reluctantly she let her arms drop. She knew instinctively that the moment of sharing had passed.

Her father turned away, sucking on his pipe. 'You'd best be going, now, love. Thank your mother for the sandwiches.'

Avril could only nod in reply, a painful lump in her throat preventing her from speaking.

★　★　★

The boarding house smelt of cabbages and beeswax. The front hall was cool and blessedly empty, giving Avril a moment to wipe her unshed tears away.

'This is a respectable boarding house.' Her mother's voice reached her from the dining room and Avril could hear a layer of disapproval barely hidden under her words. She hoped the recipient couldn't sense it. She cringed inwardly.

'The door is locked at ten pm prompt and there are to be no female visitors. Breakfast, luncheon and dinner are served at these times on the card, not a moment later. Rent must be paid a month in advance. I trust you will be happy with that?'

Avril strained to hear the reply. A man's deep voice, polite and calm. She tiptoed closer to the dining room and leaned her ear against the door. With a rush of air, the door suddenly opened and she found herself staring up into a pair of the clearest green eyes she'd ever seen. A brief expression of amusement flickered across the man's face but when she dared look back up at him, it was gone.

He was very tall. Avril was of average height, but beside him she felt petite. His unusual green eyes were set in a classically handsome face with strong cheekbones, and made her think of heroes in the films she liked to watch. His fair hair was cut short in a military style.

But there was nothing dramatic or swashbuckling about him. Instead there was an air of stillness, of restraint. He was impeccably dressed in a dark, woollen suit with a subdued checkered waistcoat and thin black tie. He held his hat in his hand as if greeting her politely.

'Avril, this is Mr Gordon Silver,' her mother said. 'Please take him and show him his room.' Her lips were pursed.

'Of course,' Avril replied, with a guilty start. She'd been staring at him rudely. What must he think of her! But another glance at him showed his features carefully set as if his momentary amusement at her had never existed.

He followed her across the hall to the upstairs room and she saw he was limping slightly. He held himself well, as though used to it, and she reckoned it was a long-standing injury — perhaps even a war wound. If her father was right about his age, then Gordon Silver could have seen war action in the last few months of 1945. He would have been very young and Avril's heart beat in sympathy at the thought of him going through such evil times. Him and all the others.

'This is your room,' she declared, gesturing expansively at the simple square space with its green-painted walls and the heavy sash window.

He walked across to the window and looked out. It was a good view. It looked across the rooftops, all slates and chimney stacks, to the wharfside warehouses and old bleaching fields, and then to the great grey-brown sluggish waters of the River Clyde in the distance.

His jaw clenched and he turned away as if displeased. Without a word he began to open a suitcase and a stack of books tumbled out onto the bed. Avril eyed them greedily.

'Goodness, what a collection. Do you like reading, then?'

Those clear green eyes settled on her and he half-smiled. 'I'm a school teacher. I've come to teach at a boys' school in the city. These are the tools of my trade.'

There was a hint of the Highlands in his accent, a way of lifting the words so that a faint melody could be heard. She liked it. She wanted to hear him speak more. But he turned away and began to line up his books on the dark mahogany dresser.

Avril slipped from the room, dismissed, it seemed. Feeling an urge to capture his likeness in a sketch, she went to find her precious notebook.

*　*　*

Gordon was tired, bone-tired. The journey from his home in a small village in the glens to Inverness, and then the long train journey to Glasgow, had taken their toll on him. His leg ached and he longed to lie down. But instead he steeled himself to the task of moving in and making the dreary room his own.

He didn't deserve to rest. If he lapsed into self-indulgence, well — the pain in his leg was a constant reminder of his guilt. The pain had lessened over the year until it was now bearable. Indeed some days he didn't notice it at all. On those days he found himself angry. He needed the pain. He deserved it for what he had done. It was a life sentence, self-imposed and righteous.

He finished stacking the books and found himself once more at the dusty window. With difficulty he managed to push the heavy painted sill upward to let in the city air. A fug of warm, fume-laden breeze came into the room. There was the taste of the dirty sea in it, wrapped in oil and carbon. No wonder the buildings were coated in blackness and grime if this was swirling around them.

Gordon looked out and across to the wide river which snaked through the city and eventually widened out beyond the city boundaries to become the sea. It was ironic and fitting that he should have to face it on a daily basis. A revulsion filled him and he turned from it. Enough for one day.

There was a letter in his pocket, where Lucille had stuffed it, crying as she hugged him goodbye. He felt for it now and pulled it out. He saw her again standing there in front of him, her pretty blue eyes reddened from her weeping, begging him not to go. Not to leave her. He had tentatively touched her long, red hair, promising nothing with his gesture.

Now he tore open her letter and ripped his heart in shreds all over again as he read her torrent of words, crammed onto the layers of thin paper.

Later he went downstairs to find the living room, intending to read the newspapers that Mrs Garnett had promised would be there. He glimpsed her daughter polishing the sideboard and hesitated to go in.

He watched her. She was slight, with a neat waist accentuated by her blue top and flaring skirt. Her dark brown hair was pulled into a high pony tail which bounced merrily as she worked. When she half-turned, Gordon noticed her pretty little nose and full mouth. Her eyes were extraordinarily dark, like pure chocolate, the black pupils nearly indistinguishable from the irises.

He felt a stirring deep within him. Something he hadn't experienced in a couple of years at least. Miss Avril Garnett was quite simply gorgeous, and she was having an intensely physical effect on him.

He'd felt his attraction for her immediately he'd opened the door of the dining room after his talk from Mrs Garnett. Avril had almost fallen onto him, and she'd clearly been eavesdropping. Her dark eyes had widened and her luscious lips were opened in a moue of surprise showing perfect white teeth. He'd found it funny, her surprise and her spying.

Hot on the heels of his amusement had come the impulse to grab her and kiss her firmly. He'd shocked himself. Luckily he had quickly found his control. He was here to work and to atone for what he had done, if that was ever possible. There were to be no distractions.

'Oh — hello.' Avril smiled, waving the polishing rag, stupidly uneasy at the sight of him, and gabbling nervously. 'Don't mind me, I'm just finishing in here. The newspapers are over there by the armchair if you want them. I can bring you a cup of tea, too.'

He nodded stiffly at her but ignored the newspapers to limp over to the window. Avril followed him, struck anew by how tall he was. The top of her head would barely graze his shoulder. He was staring out to the narrow gap between the houses where the shipyards and the busy scene of barges and tugboats and steamers could just be glimpsed.

'It's the same view as from your window,' she said, grinning. 'You can't escape from the river, I'm afraid. In fact, if you'd like to, I can show you a lovely walk. There's a tiny stream goes past the house. You can't see it because it's all closed over with the road and the slabs. But you can hear it babbling underneath. I always feel so sad for it trapped down there, but it gets free as it reaches the river. Then it sounds really happy as it rushes off to join the other water. Anyway,' she paused shyly, 'I could show you. There's a path all the way down to the edge of the river. It's marvellous to stand there and watch the boats.'

He took a step back from her, his face blanched. A shudder of repulsion contorted him. Without a word he turned on his heel and limped stiffly away. She heard his footsteps pause in the hallway, then fade away onto the stairs.

Well! If that was how he reacted to a friendly gesture, she wanted nothing more to do with him. What a rude man. In future she would ignore him as much as possible.

3

'Oooh, look who's down there talking to your Davey,' Peggy remarked, leaning against the wall of Avril's bedroom and looking out through the glass.

Peggy was Avril's best friend. She lived next door and was always popping in for a chat and to share the latest gossip. It was hot in the bedroom, and Avril wished they could go to the small park nearby. For some reason, probably its size, it had escaped being dug up in the war and was still a haven of cut green grass and colourful flowerbeds. The orange marigolds, red nasturtiums and old-fashioned poppies were in flower and Avril longed to walk beside them and drink in their beauty and their promise of summer.

Sadly, walking was not one of Peggy's enthusiasms. Avril envied Mr Gordon Silver whom she'd seen escaping the boarding house early that morning, ready to take up his new job. He was smartly dressed in a suit and hat, every inch the school master. Not that she cared what he did or where he went. She had only spoken to him to be civil in the few days that had passed since he arrived. If he was upset by her coldness to him, he didn't show it. Instead, to her pique, he appeared almost relieved. Unfortunately, he was starting to intrigue her. His air of mystery was beguiling. She put him out of her mind and concentrated on her friend.

'Who's talking to Davey?' She joined Peggy at the window.

'It's Jack Lafferty. Imagine that.' Peggy made a little moue of surprise with her bright red lips and gave Avril space to look.

Avril's bedroom was at the back of the house and the view was down to the back garden. It wasn't huge, but her mother had made it nice with a lawn and edge shrubs. There was a bench and chairs which the family rarely had time to use, but it was part of Linda Garnett's vision of summertime living.

Avril saw Davey and his ever-present guitar at the bench. He should have been at work, but had woken up ill with a splitting headache. Her mother was adamant he was not to work while he was sick, and insisted he stay at home — to be mollycoddled, in Avril's opinion.

Her mother didn't try to hide the fact that Davey was her favourite. It didn't bother Avril, because she knew she was Dad's favourite. As for the twins, they didn't seem to notice or care, so wrapped up as they were in each other.

Her gaze switched to the other figure chatting to him. It was a man — somewhat older than her brother, she guessed, maybe in his late twenties or even thirty. He was wearing a dark suit with buttoned waistcoat, and her attention was drawn to his shoes which were incredibly shiny with pointed toes. His hair was brown and too long, slicked back with oil onto his head.

At that moment he looked up as if sensing her watching. He wasn't handsome, his face was too fleshy for that, but his eyes twinkled with mischief and even from a distance Avril could sense his dangerous charm.

'Who is Jack Lafferty?' she whispered.

Peggy laughed. 'He has that effect on all the girls, Avril. Don't get carried away. He's not your type.'

'Is he yours?' Avril shot back. She rather thought he was. Peggy was loud and exuberant; popular with the boys, and knew it. She accentuated her assets with tight tops and wasp-waisted dresses and skirts. She wore a lot of make-up and had cropped her hair really short in the latest style.

Needless to say, Avril's mother disapproved of her. But Peggy was kind-hearted and fun and Avril was very fond of her.

Peggy shook her head. 'He's not my type. He's handsome enough and devilish enough. But . . . there's something about him. I don't know.' She

44

shrugged. Deep thinking and self-awareness were not Peggy's strong points. 'Come on, let's go down and I'll introduce you. My brother Johnny's a friend of Jack's. Jack manages music bands, and Johnny's in a swing band as you know.'

Avril was glad to escape the stuffiness of the house. Outside the sun was shining and she squinted against the reflections.

'Hello Jack, Davey, what are you boys up to?' Peggy greeted them cheerily.

Avril saw Davey blush. He was completely smitten with Peggy, but to no avail. She had too many more exciting offers to consider Davey Garnett.

'Peggy, my girl,' Jack answered easily. 'And who's your lovely friend?' His eyes were directly on Avril's and she felt her cheeks warm under his bold stare. He had a hungry, wolfish grin and crooked teeth that only added to his attractiveness. She felt tingly as if his eyes were stroking her as they fell to her chest and

45

waist before fixing on her face again.

'This is Avril, my sister,' Davey introduced her. His voice was eager to please. Avril wondered if Jack was offering for Davey's music band.

'Well, well, Davey boy. You didn't tell me you had a beautiful sister,' Jack answered.

Now Avril began to grow irritated. He was making her uncomfortable with his exaggerated compliments. He noticed her frown and quickly said, 'I'm sorry if I've overstepped the mark. No offence intended. Tell you what — ' he paused, hands loosely hooked in his jacket pockets, a cigarette slung now between his lips — 'I'll make it up to you. How about I take you two ladies for an ice-cream?'

Avril was torn. The day was hot and she adored ice-cream. But there was a sense of danger about Jack Lafferty. What would her mother say if she knew Avril was with him? Her mother had an unerring sense of what was right and proper, and Avril could tell right away that Jack would fall short of the line.

'Davey?' she asked.

'Davey can't come, can you, old mate?' Jack said firmly, with a sympathetic smile. 'He's not well. He's under strict instructions to sit still here and be looked after by his mum.'

Davey flushed a deeper shade of red but Peggy was already down the path to the side of the house, hips swaying provocatively as she teetered in her new sandals. Avril wished desperately that she had new heels. She was conscious of her girlish dress and wished she'd worn her new skirt that day.

She picked up her gloves and hat in the house and found Jack and Peggy sitting in a very flash car outside. Jack leapt out to open the passenger door and her nostrils were assailed by the scents of the interior leather upholstery and stale cigarette smoke. Jack's fingertips brushed her cheek accidentally as he politely ushered her in, and she felt the trail of his touch burn into her skin. She felt suddenly alive and excited at the potential of the day.

They drove through the city until Jack pulled to an abrupt halt, causing the car behind to blast its horn.

Unconcerned, he hopped out and led the way to an Italian ice-cream parlour with a shiny metal counter and high, pastel-coloured stools. The jukebox was playing Perry Como and a couple of girls were giggling in a corner booth and swaying to the beat of the music. They nudged one another when they saw Jack. He ignored them and the three of them slid into a booth beside the window. The air was scented with vanilla and fruit syrups and the sharp, rich roast of coffee beans. Avril sat down with a satisfied sigh. This was wonderful.

* * *

Jack Lafferty was pleased with himself. A couple of nifty deals had turned out very nicely indeed and he was flush. He fingered the notes appreciatively, feeling the thickness of the wad, as he paid for the ice creams. Life was good and — when he looked at Avril Garnett — he felt it was sure to get even better. She was sexy and didn't even know it. Her creamy, flawless skin made him ache to touch it. He'd managed to do so when she got into the car and had clocked her reaction. She liked him too; he was sure of it. She might fight it but the attraction was there.

He sat down at the table and the waitress brought the ices over, served in tall glasses with long spoons and dripping in raspberry sauce. He wasn't a great fan of ice cream, preferring stronger delights, but he'd got himself one anyway.

Avril smiled her thanks sweetly at him and Jack felt his chest tighten. She had no idea how pretty she was — those large, dark eyes with their black fringe of lashes and that full and temptingly kissable soft mouth.

Beside her Peggy was in full flow with some dull story or other. Her head was thrown back with loud laughter and she clutched a lit cigarette in her fingers. She was harmless enough, but too brassy for Jack's taste. He got the impression that she didn't fancy him either, so that was all right. He didn't want any competition when it came to hunting Avril.

'So what do you do, Jack?' He was even besotted with her voice. It was soft and cultured for a Glasgow accent. Just right.

'Yeah Jack, tell Avril what you do for a living,' Peggy mocked, cocking an eyebrow in challenge.

Jack shifted in his seat. Peggy knew too much from her brother Johnny.

'A bit of this, a bit of that,' he said vaguely, lighting another cigarette and letting it dangle from his lower lip. It gave him a moody look, he liked to think. The ladies usually went for it. But now he caught Avril's cool stare and hastily stubbed it out, remembering how she'd declined the offer of a cigarette earlier.

'Actually I manage music bands,' he said, making an effort.

'That sounds interesting,' Avril replied, her tone envious.

'Yes, it's that, all right,' Jack agreed. He could have added that it may be interesting but the pay was lousy. He had to resort to his other work to get paid decently. There was always a market for rationed goods if you knew where to look. It was just a shame that the government was rapidly taking so many items off ration. Still, there were things people needed and Jack Lafferty was just the man to provide them.

'Do you like dancing?' he asked, suddenly inspired.

Avril smiled. 'Very much. Peggy and I go regularly to the Locarno, don't we, Pegs?'

'I'm sure we wouldn't find Jack there,' Peggy said snidely. 'It's a bit tame for him.'

Jack laughed, unabashed. 'I've got a coupla swing bands playing at Telfers in a fortnight's time. Would you like to go and dance there? It's a great atmosphere.'

'Yes, we would like to go — wouldn't we, Peggy?' Avril said quickly. She gave Jack a warm look which had his heart beating faster. He managed to brush his hand against hers under the pretext of moving her empty glass. There it was, a spark of electricity which leaped between them. Her eyes widened. She snatched her hand away as if burnt by a match. But her gaze met his steadily.

She was like fire burning under ice. Her cool exterior was prim and proper but Jack imagined melting the ice and letting the tigress free. A busy dance hall would be just the ticket.

He slapped his thigh with enthusiasm. 'Great — that's settled, then.'

Peggy looked surprised at Avril's agreement but shrugged.

Avril jumped up suddenly, pointing to the wall clock. 'Sorry, I'll have to go. I promised my mother I'd help her make the dinners for the lodgers.'

In Jack's opinion, Mrs Garnett could

wait. But he remembered in time that he was being a perfect gentleman. He stood up too. 'Of course. No problem. I'll run you both home.'

Could he risk another gesture which would bring him into bodily contact with Avril? He was a gambler by nature, but Jack knew when to stop. So he kept his hands to himself and drove sedately back to the boarding house. He mock-saluted them as a farewell and drove off.

* * *

Avril's emotions were in turmoil. When Jack had touched her hand briefly, a tingle had shot straight up her arm and her insides had turned liquid hot. How could he have such an effect on her?

She'd even been jealous of Peggy, her best friend. Peggy made socialising appear so easy. She laughed well and told clever, entertaining tales. She was confident and stylish. All the things Avril was not. Had she imagined, then,

Jack's interest in her? How could such a sophisticated man be intrigued by a girl like her? Yet he'd been moved by their contact too. She would've sworn to it.

Arriving home, she took off her hat and gloves in the hallway. Peggy followed her in.

'Well, that was an interesting afternoon,' she drawled. 'Let me see.' She spun Avril round as if searching for something.

Avril was perplexed. 'What is it? What are you looking for?'

'I'm looking for what Jack Lafferty sees in you.'

'Oh!' Avril gasped, her hands covering her mouth.

'I'm not blind,' Peggy went on. 'Jack's besotted by you. I've never seen him so attentive to any one particular girl. He's charming to all the girls, but you . . . it's different, somehow. I'm just amazed, I wouldn't have said you were his type.' Peggy stopped, then added kindly, 'You know I love you, Avril. You're my best friend. But you're a homely sort, we both know that. You're not glamorous or sophisticated.'

It hurt a little to hear it said so plainly, but Avril had to admit it was true. She was literally the girl-next-door. Fresh and wholesome. Those descriptions should be positive and proud but all of a sudden she hated them. She wanted to be beautiful and well-dressed and confident.

'But Jack likes me. You're sure?' Avril asked.

Peggy laughed. 'I'd say so. But don't ask me why. And Avril . . . ' She paused, suddenly serious. 'Take care, okay?'

'Of course, silly. There's nothing to worry about,' Avril reassured her. Inside, her heart was dancing. She'd wished for a more exciting life, and here, it had tumbled into her lap. She'd take care, but she wasn't going to let this opportunity slip away.

* * *

Peggy stayed to chat in Avril's room and it wasn't until she smelled the stew cooking that Avril remembered her promise to her mother.

'Sorry Peggy, I said I would help make the lodgers' dinners. Mum says I've a knack of making the meat go further. Silly tricks with vegetables, that's all.'

'I like your mum,' Peggy remarked unexpectedly. 'She copes really well, doesn't she? It can't be easy for her, what with your dad being invalided and her having to support the whole family. She could have so easily gone the way of my mum.'

Peggy's mother was much too fond of a bottle, which was why Peggy was so often to be found at the boarding house. They didn't usually speak about her mother, Avril out of respect and Peggy out of embarrassment. Avril didn't like to tell Peggy that her mother disapproved of her, thinking her too loud and cheap-looking. It was worse, now that Peggy had admired and complimented Linda.

'Mum works hard,' Avril agreed. 'But I wish she'd relax a bit more. It can be hard to live up to her expectations sometimes.'

'But at least she has expectations of you,' Peggy argued. 'My Mum doesn't care what I do.'

'Oh Peggy, I'm sure that's not true,' Avril cried out, hugging her friend.

Peggy pushed her off playfully. 'Oi, you'll crumple my clothes, you daftie. Enough of my wallowing. Do you think I could help you in the kitchen?'

Avril wondered what her mother would say to that. But Peggy's comments had made her think. It never occurred to her that Mum carried such a heavy burden. Besides, Dad was there too. It wasn't like poor Peggy's situation; her father had been killed in the war.

Peggy gave a low unladylike whistle. 'Who is that utterly stunning young man?'

Avril followed Peggy's hungry gaze,

although she'd already guessed who she meant. Gordon Silver had arrived back from his first day as schoolmaster in his new job. He had taken off his hat and set down his briefcase. He looked tired, Avril thought. His fair hair was ruffled from the hat and his green eyes were creased. She quelled any compassion.

'Is that your new lodger?' Peggy was whispering loudly. 'You never told me he was young. You never said he was the most handsome man I'm ever going to meet. Avril, you have to introduce me.'

'I could introduce you,' Avril answered in her frostiest tone. 'But it would be a waste of your time and of mine. He is a very disagreeable person and likely to ignore you completely.'

She noted with satisfaction from Gordon's tightened jaw and the slight rise of colour in his cheeks that her arrow had landed perfectly on target.

Avril spun on her heel and marched into the kitchen, dragging a reluctant Peggy with her.

* * *

The dinner preparation was not a success. Linda Garnett was of the opinion that too many cooks spoil the broth and Peggy was put to peeling potatoes and chopping carrots. She was disgruntled and showed it. Avril was given the superior task of preparing the stew which had to feed nine people. Linda slipped in a generous helping of dumplings to make it go further.

'When, oh when will meat rationing stop?' she huffed, raising a warning eyebrow when it looked as if Peggy might dare to answer.

'It's annoying but it can't be long now,' Avril soothed, stirring in the dumplings and sprinkling seasoning onto the stew. 'Shall I serve up?'

She carefully carried out the hot plates of food. Mrs Petrocelli and Mr Phillips both looked hopeful so she served them first. Gordon was sitting by himself at the corner table. She took him his plate and laid it down. He had no fork so she went to find one. As she put it down, he grabbed her wrist gently but firmly. Surprised, she met his gaze.

'I wanted to apologise,' Gordon said tightly. 'I think I was rather rude to you the day we met. I'd like to start afresh. Perhaps we could be friends?'

Avril was not one to bear a grudge for long. To be honest, it was a relief to finish with cold-shouldering him. She and Gordon lived in the same house, it would be better if they got along.

'Yes, I'd like that,' she said simply.

He looked pleased and began to eat his dinner with vigour as though relieved of a small burden.

What Avril didn't understand, as she lay in bed that night staring at the ceiling, was why his grasp of her wrist should send an electric shock running through her system, when it was Jack whom she liked.

4

Avril had borrowed Peggy's new white shoes. They had low, narrow heels and a pretty ribboned bow at the toes. She was conscious of the stickiness of the black soil as she carefully trotted along the home-made paths of the allotment. She was wearing her favourite navy blue dress with the white polka dots and a broad, blue belt cinched in at the waist. Her hat, gloves and handbag were all white too, perfectly accessorised for this bright, airy Saturday lunchtime.

Inside she was burning with excitement and impatience for the afternoon. Peggy had passed her a note from Jack inviting her out to afternoon tea. But first, she had to take her father his lunch in the traditional manner.

The earth had suddenly given up its secrets in the last few days, and everywhere the regimented rows of plots were furred with green as the shoots of new growth broke through. Avril was humming a snatch of Davey's Nat King Cole favourite when she came to an abrupt halt. An unusual scene met her eyes.

Instead of the shed with its half-open door and familiar curl of smoke, there was real activity on the plot. Her father was outside, leaning on a gardening fork and pointing at a patch of earth. His hat was pushed back on his head, giving him a curiously rakish look.

Yet what jolted Avril the most was the sight of his companion. Gordon was there on her father's hallowed space. Not only that, he was digging in the plot. He was dressed in beige trousers and an open-necked shirt and his fair hair was tousled from the breeze. Avril noticed that his limp was hardly there at all when he moved. The two men were talking so intently that they didn't see Avril until she was right there beside them.

'I hope that's lunch, we're starving,'

was her father's opening greeting. He looked better today, his cheeks ruddy from the fresh air and his eyes twinkling.

'You're not overdoing it, Dad, are you?' Avril asked.

'Nonsense, love. I've got a great helper in Gordon here. I'm directing operations, that's all.' He laughed heartily which ended in a rackety cough.

'Perhaps we deserve a break,' Gordon suggested smoothly, bringing a chair out onto the slabbed area for the older man.

Avril shot him a look of approval. For a second there was an answering gleam in his eyes but it was dampened quickly.

'Show Avril the bird's nest,' David suggested. He sounded so happy, and Avril realised it was Gordon's presence. Her dad was keen for Davey to show an appreciation of gardening, but it wasn't Davey's hobby. He was entirely engrossed in his music. Here, though, was a companion who shared his enthusiasm for living things.

'It's over here in the hedge,' Gordon said.

She followed him to the line of burgeoning hawthorn sprigged with green leaves and white blossom. He parted the branches gingerly, avoiding the sharp spikes. Inside in a hollow of leaves was a blackbird's nest complete with three pale blue eggs.

'Where's the mother?' Avril whispered. She was aware of Gordon's nearness. He was so close that she could feel his body heat. She saw golden bristles on his jaw, captured by the light, and for a fleeting moment wondered how it would feel to touch them. He was careful not to bump into her as they left the nest. At the top of a nearby birch tree, the blackbird scolded them with chirps and screeches.

'That answers your question.' He laughed. She was caught by the richness of it. A momentary joy that he cut off.

Gordon started to dig. Avril tried not

to notice how his shoulder muscles rippled under his shirt and the strength of his thighs as he plunged the spade deep into the earth.

'Have you got an allotment at home?' she called, standing on the path and trying to push off a streak of dirt from one shoe, using the other.

He stopped and leaned on the spade handle, his skin flushed with exertion. 'There's no need for allotments where I come from. Food's reasonably plentiful from the farms. Nature's abundant.' He stopped himself and his face shuttered. 'Besides, this is my home now.'

Avril felt a shaft of disappointment. Why did he clam up so, every time it looked as if he might relax and warm up? It was as if he remembered himself and snap! Back to a stiffness and formality more suited to a much older man.

She shared out the sandwiches. There were two extra chairs at the back of the shed for when Bert and his pal came to visit. Gordon set them out. They sat

65

companionably in a semi-circle facing the plots. There was an easiness to Gordon when he remembered to relax, Avril decided. If only she could ignore the length of his leg stretched out beside her. He was oblivious to it, but she was acutely conscious of the fact that her skirt had brushed his trouser leg. Silly, really. There was nothing to it. Nothing unseemly.

'And who is this lovely lady?' David Garnett piped up in a jolly tone.

Avril looked up to see her mother walking briskly towards them. She was dressed for going out. The rayon house coat and work scarf were gone. Instead she was neat and tidy in a roll-neck top and long pinafore dress with her buttoned jacket over it. She had on her hat and gloves and carried a patent leather clasped handbag.

It was her Saturday lunchtime garb. The one time in the week which Linda took for herself. She was a member of a local Ladies Luncheon Club. On Saturday lunchtimes, the lodgers had to fend for themselves. This bewildered Mrs Petrocelli and Mr Phillips every week anew, so Avril normally stepped in to feed them. Today she'd begged and bullied Davey into doing it. A frisson of excitement went through her as she remembered Jack and their date this afternoon.

'Away with you, David Garnett. What nonsense,' Linda returned shortly, but Avril could tell his compliment had pleased her. Her mother's dark eyes were bright and a slight smile twitched her lipsticked lips. Avril saw her then with a flash of objectivity. She would have been a pretty girl. Her hair was iron-grey now, but had been dark brown. Her skin was creased with lines especially around the eyes and mouth, but it was not hard to imagine it clear with youth. It wasn't difficult, then, to see what David Garnett had seen in her. Before the war, before the hardship and daily grind and invalidity, theirs must have been a happy marriage, she supposed. It was there in her father's teasing compliment and the brightness of her mother's eyes.

'Mr Silver, I see my husband has you slaving over his vegetable plot. I hope he hasn't bullied you into helping?'

'Please, Mrs Garnett, call me Gordon. And I'm very happy to help. It's given me a chance to talk about my father and hear stories of what he did in the war. I'm most grateful to Mr Garnett for that.'

Avril and her mother were shocked to silence. Dad, who would not speak of the war to them, had opened up to a stranger. *How would Mum feel about that?* Avril wondered.

But she'd underestimated her mother's character. Linda smiled at Gordon with real warmth. It flowed over him as acceptance.

'That's wonderful, Gordon. Just wonderful.'

She stared away to the far gate, blinking twice before coming back to them, all brisk business once more. 'I was thinking that we need to discuss

68

the Queen's Coronation. It's next month and we must celebrate. Glasgow is the second city of the Empire, after all.'

'What had you in mind?' Dad asked warily. If it involved him not sitting in his allotment shed, that was going to be a problem.

'What about a street party?' Avril interrupted with enthusiasm. 'There could be food and music and dancing. I'm sure if we asked the neighbours, they'd help.'

'Well,' Linda said slowly. 'That might work. If all the women cooked and baked, we'd have a feast. We could save our ration coupons.'

'I would be glad to help with decorations or heavy lifting,' Gordon offered. He looked interested. Avril smiled at him encouragingly. His face closed. *What on earth is the matter with him?* she thought, exasperated. One minute he was involved and enthusiastic, the next he was withdrawn. But why should she care anyway? She was more interested in engaging with Jack. Let Gordon Silver be mysterious if he wanted.

'I shall take the idea to the luncheon club,' Linda declared. 'I'm sure there'll be a good response.'

There was a silence between them. A good, rich silence of people at one with each other. The female blackbird spoiled it by ratcheting up her warning call as a mangy ginger cat slunk out of the bushes.

'What are you all dressed up for?' Linda demanded of Avril suspiciously. 'Are you going out?'

Avril squirmed. She hadn't meant for her mother to see her sneaking off to meet Jack. Not that she was doing anything wrong, exactly. It was just that Mum's radar was twitchy and razor-sharp.

'Yes, I am. Or I might be. I was considering it,' she mumbled.

She smoothed the arm of her glove. Unfortunately she glanced at Gordon. His eyes were crinkled with amusement.

She had the impulse to laugh with him. Honestly, her mother treated her as if she were twelve, like the twins. She was a woman of twenty-one! If she was married, she'd be in charge of her own house and able to do what she liked. But while she was under her parents' roof, she had to obey their rules. It was drilled into all of them. She sighed inwardly.

'I'm running late now.' Linda shook her head, exasperated. 'It's my turn to run the knitting bee, too. Where have Gloria and Shirley disappeared to? I said they could come along and knit.'

As if on cue, a girl in a yellow sundress came flying helter-skelter up the path to stand panting in front of them. In her hand was clutched the ubiquitous bag of sweets and she was chewing on something. It was evidently licorice strip because when she opened her mouth to speak, her teeth and tongue were black.

'Shirley Garnett!' Linda said severely. 'You have the manners of a monkey. How many times have I told you about not eating in the street? And just look at the state of your hair. Did you even brush it?'

Shirley cast her merry blue eyes down. She was unquashed by her mother's scolding, but she played along. It was easier that way.

'Now, where's Gloria? We have to get going. At this rate there will be no lunch left.'

Shirley fidgeted, hopping from one foot to the other.

'Gloria's not coming. She's lying down reading.'

Avril knew she was lying. Shirley always hopped about when she lied. It was a dead giveaway. But Linda didn't know that. And the word 'reading' was inspired. If Gloria wasn't to knit, then at least she was spending her time productively. Avril wondered what she was really up to.

'Very well — let's go.' Linda steered her youngest child in the direction of the gate.

Avril made her farewells too, eager to

see Jack. She went back to the boarding house to wait and to tidy up. Peggy's shoes needed a wipe down and she wanted to brush her hair again.

As she passed by the table in the hallway she saw that Gordon had received a letter. Curious, she picked it up. He got a letter almost every other day. She'd seen him, too, going out to the telephone kiosk a block away. Was he telephoning the person who wrote so persistently to him?

She read the address as if it could tell her. The handwriting was rounded and thick as though heavily pressed into the paper. It was a girl's writing, Avril thought. A girlfriend — or a sister, or an acquaintance? She propped it up carefully on the table against the wall where he would see it when he came in. It was none of her business.

★ ★ ★

Avril waited nervously for Jack. She stood clutching her handbag, on the doorstep of the house. Her pulse was going like a hammer and she felt faint.

She forced herself to breathe in and out. *Relax*, she told herself. *It's only afternoon tea*. But her senses were heightened. She was energised and ready. Jack was late. What if he wasn't coming? She began to doubt the note. Perhaps it hadn't been today. Had she got the date wrong? Or the time?

Just as she was about to go inside and find the note to check, Jack turned up. He was walking today; no sign of the car. He was dapper in his suit and had crammed a hat onto his head. His shoes, if anything, were shinier than before.

He whistled appreciatively when he saw Avril. 'Well, don't you look nice.'

'Hello, Jack. I was beginning to think you weren't going to show up.' Avril couldn't help a faint note of reproof.

He had the good grace to look ashamed. 'Car troubles,' he explained with a wave of his hand. He offered the crook of his arm to her gallantly. People would take them for a real couple, Avril thought proudly, as they headed out of Aline Street along into the shopping streets.

Peggy's shoes made a dainty clatter as she walked, and she knew she looked good. Jack certainly seemed to think so. He took every opportunity to glance at her wolfishly.

She ignored a tiny ripple of unease. Jack was a gentleman. He was a friend of Peggy's. What could possibly happen? No, it was fine. She was inexperienced with men; she'd never had a steady boyfriend. But that didn't matter. She was ready for experience. Ready for fun. Ready for life.

'Where would you like to go?' Jack asked.

'In there?' Avril said, pointing to a tea shop they were about to pass. It was an old-fashioned sort of place which would serve high teas on lace doilies. Inside, through the street window, she could see ladies her mother's age in their Saturday hats, drinking from china teacups and sharing tiny cakes from tiered cake stands.

But Jack pulled her on. 'What about over there instead?' He nodded. On the opposite side of the street was a Spanish-style coffee bar. Music was leaking out onto the street. An older couple, walking arm-in-arm, shook their heads as they went by. It looked busy inside with young people. Jack pushed open the door and held it for Avril to go in.

There was a hiss of steam from a huge metal espresso coffee machine and the juke box was on. The music blended with the chatter of the customers into a thick wall of sound. It was lively and fun. Avril, pleased, found a free table for them beside the window. Jack shrugged his shoulders inside his jacket uncomfortably.

'Are you okay?' she asked.

'Sure, sure. Let's order,' he answered, pulling his collar away from his neck with a finger. He was clearly ill at ease. Avril vowed silently to be relaxing and entertaining company.

The waitress came to take their orders. Avril chose an ice cream sundae while Jack went for a double espresso and an Italian biscuit.

'Thank you for inviting me out,' Avril said guilelessly. She was genuinely grateful.

Jack focused on her and his eyes were lively. His face relaxed. He was more like the Jack she'd met a few days before.

'I wanted to see you again. You know why, don't you?' he teased.

'I think so,' she answered, confused. She was glad when the waitress arrived back with their food and drink. The full blast of Jack's attention could be too strong.

'So tell me about you,' she suggested swiftly, to dilute the atmosphere. 'Have you any family?'

He downed his espresso in one throw and called for another. Avril took a small spoonful of her sundae and waited.

'Family? You don't want to hear about that.' The wolfish grin was back. His teeth looked sharp. He lit a cigarette, then stubbed it out immediately, remembering her distaste for the habit.

'Yes, I do,' she encouraged.

'Okay. If you really do. There isn't much to tell. There's just me and my old man. My Ma took off years ago. Don't blame her.' He chuckled mirthlessly. 'The old man's a handful. Still, he's taught me a few tricks over the years.'

'Tricks? What do you mean?'

'Well, you know,' Jack shifted in his seat, glancing past her out of the window, then back to her. 'How to make a living. We worked together during the war on various projects. I'm a Londoner born and bred,' he added proudly.

'Were you in reserved occupations during the war?' Avril asked, trying to make sense of it.

'You could say that,' he replied

evasively with another glance out of the window.

'Are you looking for someone?'

'What? No! No. Where was I?'

'Being a Londoner, born and bred,' Avril prompted drily.

'Had to get out rather suddenly, opportunities up here in the North. So here I am'.' Jack smiled, relieved to have finished his story. But Avril was intent on finding out more about him.

'Do you have any brothers or sisters?'

'I've an older sister. She married a Yank and scarpered over there. Can't say I blame her.' Jack finished his second espresso and offered her the biscuit. She was pleased. She nibbled it, savouring its nutty sweetness. It was intimate, sharing food. A lover's gesture.

Jack jumped up. 'Sorry, need to make a phone call. Back in a mo.' His movements were jerky, his gaze darting about the shop. Too much strong coffee, she guessed. He leaned over the counter and the boy handed him the telephone.

Avril ate the rest of the biscuit idly. Outside the coffee bar window, two men huddled together. There was an air of menace about them. One was talking rapidly. Avril saw he was missing his front teeth. His friend was short and squat, reminding her of a warty toad. His striped suit was in bad taste and his face was hidden by the brim of his hat. They pushed open the door and came in. With alarm, she saw them clock Jack and make their way towards him. Jack held up his hands, palms out.

Avril half-rose anxiously. She should help him. But it was ridiculous. They were in the middle of a busy coffee shop. What could these men possibly do? Yet even as she had this reassuring thought, the two of them sidled Jack from the phone and out of the door.

Avril froze. Around her, the noise and laughter continued unabated. It was strange. No one had noticed a thing. Jack had been kidnapped in broad daylight under a crowd's nose, so to speak. A bubble of hysteria welled up in her.

Just as she was about to scream, Jack reappeared and slid back into the chair across from her, attempting an air of nonchalance. But he was pale. His hand shook as he lit a cigarette and she didn't try to stop him. He drew heavily on it.

'Jack? Jack, are you all right? Who were those men?'

He shook his head. 'Come on, let's go. I'll take you home.'

He kept off the main street, leading her down narrow side lanes until they reached the river walkway. Nothing could disguise the sluggish brown-grey pollution, nor mask the pervasive stink which rose up from the surface of the water. But all along the walkway, bluebells and tiny ornamental leeks had sprung up. Little signs of hope.

The path wound along faithfully beside the riverbank and would lead them back to the boarding house via Avril's secret stream. A fat bee clung to a bluebell's clustered petals.

Jack had recovered his confidence. He walked jauntily, telling Avril about his latest band booking. She watched as his polished shoe came down, crushing the bluebells. The bee flew off.

They reached the boarding house without further incident. Avril let out a breath she hadn't known she was holding, and let Jack say goodbye on the street. She didn't want to have to explain anything to her mother.

He went off, whistling. Avril turned to skip up the steps, only to see Gordon there, evidently ready to go out. He must have seen her with Jack. The thought made her feel strange. Especially as the look on his face was one of disappointment.

5

Avril had to admire her friend. Peggy was pulling out all the stops trying to engage Gordon's interest. Her lips were painted cherry-red and she was wearing a pair of paste pearl earrings which Avril hadn't seen before. They suited her cropped blonde hair and low-necked top. She was leaning forward at the table, giving Gordon the best view possible of her cleavage. To his credit, he was admirably restrained. His responses were polite and friendly, but nothing more.

They were sitting chatting in the large, comfortable living room. The curtains were drawn against the dusk and a low fire crackled in the hearth, despite the time of year. The old house never lost a faint dampness even in high summer, and Linda was forever battling to dry out the air.

'I'm sooo bored,' Peggy sighed, drawing out the words exaggeratedly. She'd given up on posturing to Gordon and was drumming her long, pink varnished fingernails on the table top.

'Thanks very much,' Avril retorted teasingly. 'It's nice to know you enjoy our company.'

It felt good including Gordon in the 'our'. Since his apology they'd got along much better, although in the main they simply said 'hello' and 'goodbye' as they passed in the hall; there wasn't much time for simply sitting. Tonight, however, Avril and Peggy had been at a loose end, unsure what to do. They'd wandered, chatting, into the living room and discovered Gordon there reading the newspaper.

'I don't mean you,' Peggy clarified hastily. 'I mean generally. I've nothing to look forward to.'

'Yes, you do,' Avril reminded her. 'The street party for the Coronation's going to be fabulous.'

'Yeah, but that's *weeks* away. I need

something *now*.' She glanced coyly at Gordon from under her lashes.

Avril hid a smile. It was very obvious that Peggy wanted Gordon to step up and ask her out on a date. When she saw him start to speak, Avril felt a forceful rush of conflicting emotions. Firstly, shock, because for some reason she didn't think Gordon liked Peggy in that way — although she didn't want to dig too deeply into why she imagined that. Then came a nasty twinge of jealousy, which was misplaced and grossly unfair of her. She didn't want Gordon — did she? — when she had Jack! So why shouldn't Peggy go out with Gordon? And finally, a cool wash of relief when she realised he wasn't asking Peggy out at all.

'Actually, I have a favour to ask of both of you.' He looked uncertain.

'Go on.' Peggy folded her hands under her chin, rapt with attention.

Avril sat quietly. Gordon looked at her, his expression unreadable.

'I'm supposed to take my class of

boys on a day trip this week, to the seaside. It's a tradition of the school, apparently, to go 'doon the watter' or down the Clyde as we would say, to the seaside towns on the Argyll coast. It gives the boys some much-needed fresh air for the lungs, and gives their long-suffering mothers a rest. I could do with a couple of willing helpers to accompany us.'

'I can't see why boys from Kelvinside would need fresh air,' Avril protested, naming a very well-off area of Glasgow. 'As for a rest from their mothers, a break from their nanny would be more likely.'

'Oh, who cares,' Peggy butted in, delighted. 'I'll come, Gordon. I don't know any small boys, but how difficult can it be? I'm sure they'll be dear wee fellows.'

Gordon frowned at Avril, his green eyes puzzled.

'Kelvinside? Where did you get that idea from? I don't work there. I teach at a poor school in the East End. I was going to warn you that the boys might be . . . harbouring . . . a few creatures in their hair. They'll be scrubbed up as best their mothers can, but there's always one or two.'

Peggy shuddered at this, but Avril was intrigued.

'I thought . . . I don't know why, I visualised you at a posh school. You look so smart going out every morning.' She blushed, realising she'd just admitted to watching him in the mornings.

Gordon's frown deepened as he challenged her. 'You don't think the boys deserve a smart teacher because they're poor?'

'Yes — no. I, I misjudged you, that's what I'm trying to say. I'm sorry,' Avril stammered, her face still flushed.

Gordon's expression softened and the glint returned to his eyes. 'It's fine, Avril. I'm sorry too. I get so used to defending my decision to work there when I could've taken up other offers from better schools. I want to make a difference. To my mind, I can do that most by teaching boys to improve themselves and to be able to beat poverty by education.'

Peggy looked from Gordon to Avril and back again. Her eyes narrowed and a little smile played on her lips. 'So, what do you want us to do?' she asked, putting her arm round Avril, making them a team. Avril pinched her waist and she squealed.

'The plan is to take the class on the train to Helensburgh, which is at the seaside. There's an open air swimming pool and they'll have a dip. Then we'll hold a sandcastle competition on the beach. The problem is that I don't swim.' Gordon tapped his injured leg. 'Would you two be prepared to chaperone them in the water?'

'We'd love to,' Avril told him. Why the notion of a day out with a bunch of rowdy school boys should make her so happy, she didn't know.

Peggy squeezed her arm in excitement and started planning aloud what they would wear and what they would pack for a picnic lunch.

'It's practically summer so we'll get away with light skirts and tops,' she decided, staring off into the distance as if already lying on a sunny beach. 'I'll have to have a good rummage for my swimsuit. I haven't worn it since last year, in fact I haven't a clue where it is. Oh, and lunch. Hard-boiled eggs for definite. They are an essential part of any picnic.'

Avril and Gordon shared a moment's amusement. His eyes were really an incredibly vivid shade of green, Avril thought. He had an arresting face because of them. A man should have a strong jaw like that, too.

Now he was looking at her strangely. She blushed. She must have been staring. What on earth was wrong with her?

'Avril? You didn't answer my question,' Peggy said petulantly.

'Sorry, I missed it.'

'How could you miss it? I'm sitting right next to you,' Peggy grumbled and shook her head in disgust. 'I was thinking tomatoes would be too messy in sandwiches so meat or fishpaste might be better.'

Avril had to hand it to her, Peggy was really getting into the swing of it. Her enthusiasm was shining through.

'Fishpaste's fine with me.'

'Great. Let me do the picnic, it'll be fun.'

'Sounds as though my suggestion has cured your boredom,' Gordon commented. He sounded almost teasing. Avril was in two minds as to whether that was a good thing or not. On the one hand, it meant Gordon was relaxing far more than she'd seen him do hitherto. But on the other hand, it could be construed as flirting. Was he flirting with Peggy? And why should she mind, anyway? What was wrong with her tonight? Her emotions were tumbling about and up and down.

'It certainly has cured me.' Peggy's eyes flashed. 'I'm up for anything now.' She twirled round the room laughing and glancing at Gordon to make sure he was watching her.

Avril built up the fire, not because it needed it but to hide her confusion. She concentrated on creating a clever pyramid of coals so that she didn't have to see Peggy firting like mad.

She'd just placed the top coal gingerly on top with the fire-blackened tongs, when the whole structure gave way. The fire spat angrily and sparks flew out of the grate. Avril shrieked as a spark hit her arm. Gordon swept it away quickly and replaced the fire guard over the uneasy flames.

'Are you okay? Are you burned?'

Avril shook her head, embarrassed. 'That was daft of me. But no, I'm fine. You were so quick, it barely landed on me before it was off again.'

Peggy had stopped mid-twirl. Her expression was unreadable but when Avril caught her gaze she smiled back stiffly.

'I need to get going. It's getting late.'

'It's not that late — please stay a

while,' Avril protested. She wasn't in the mood for turning in yet. She was restless and wide awake.

'Mum'll be needing my help. She's a little poorly today,' Peggy said tartly, gathering her handbag and her shoes which she'd kicked off.

'I'm sorry to hear that,' Avril replied. She knew that Peggy's mother was most likely not ill at all, but suffering the effects of too much drink. All of a sudden, she felt bad about feeling jealous of Peggy and Gordon. Why shouldn't Peggy flirt and have fun? She had a miserable home life. She deserved to be as happy as she could outside it.

'We'll have a great time at the seaside together,' she said sincerely, hugging her friend. She waved Peggy off and saw her nip in through her own door before she bolted the house shut and went back to the living room.

Gordon hadn't moved and she was glad. He wasn't ready to retire either, it seemed. The fire had calmed to glowing coals and grey ashes. It gave off a good heat to the room. Avril tucked her legs up under her in the armchair.

'It's kind of you both to agree to help on the trip,' Gordon commented, rather formally.

'Not at all, we'll be glad to,' Avril returned equally politely. There was a silence. It struck her that they'd never been alone together for any length of time. She didn't know him.

It must have struck him as a lengthening silence too because he asked, 'Have you always lived here?' as if making after dinner conversation. Well, she could play along.

'Not always, no. Mum and Dad bought the boarding house after he was invalided out at the end of the war. It was my Mum's idea; she felt she could support us by taking in lodgers when it was obvious that Dad wouldn't be able to work.'

'She's a strong woman, your mother,' Gordon remarked, and there was respect in his voice as he echoed Peggy's admiration of Linda Garnett.

'Yes, she is, though I never thought of her that way,' Avril admitted. 'Growing up, I was too busy being annoyed by her rules and her expectations of me. The only time I escaped that was when I was evacuated during the war.'

'Where did you go?'

'Mum was terrified the Germans would blitz Glasgow so she sent me to her sister who lived on a farm in the Borders. Her other sister took Gloria and Shirley. Davey got to stay at home.'

'That must have been lonely,' Gordon observed. He leaned forward in his armchair, listening.

For some reason, Avril told the truth for the first time about that episode in her life.

'I wasn't lonely — not one bit.'

There, it was out. He would be horrified at her callousness. But when she looked at him she saw only interest and empathy.

'It sounds terrible, and you're the first person I've confessed that to. But I didn't miss my family at all for the six weeks I was away. By then Mum was desperate for us all to return. It's hard to explain. I must sound like an awful, cold-hearted person, but I felt free. Growing up as one of four children, there's never any space or peace, or anything to call your own. Everything naturally has to be shared. But there on Aunt Sellie's farm, I could just be me.'

Avril shifted on her chair, wanting to explain properly, to make him understand. 'Aunt Sellie is the eccentric of the family, the black sheep. She treated me like an adult and spoke to me as one. I was given space to think about things.'

That was when she'd started to write. But she wasn't ready to share that with Gordon. It was too personal and too tender.

She went on, 'The farm was huge and I was allowed to roam for miles. I was exploring every day and it was so exciting. There was such a sense of freedom, like I'd never experienced before and never have since.'

'And then you had to come home,' Gordon prompted.

'Mum was missing us all. She couldn't bear us to be away any longer. As it was, we didn't get bombed anyway. Funnily, the moment I saw them all again, Mum and Davey and the twins, I realised how much I'd missed them. I cried and cried, couldn't stop. Mum still tells the story of my homecoming tears.'

'You must have bottled it all up while you were away. It's a form of denial,' Gordon suggested.

'Yes, that could be what it was,' Avril agreed in surprise, considering the idea. 'I never thought of that. I always blamed myself for not feeling enough.' She smiled at him. 'It was an unusual episode in my life. I still crave a similar experience. In a way, I'm waiting for life to start. There must be more to it than this.' She gestured at the quiet room with its heavy, sombre drapes and old-fashioned furniture. A puff of air rattled down the chimney making the embers glow.

'I could tell you that life is what you make of it,' Gordon said, with a short, humourless laugh. 'But perhaps you shouldn't be so ready to throw away what you have.'

Avril wanted to ask what he meant but his face was suddenly shut in. He'd withdrawn from her, and she wanted him back.

'So what about you? Where did you grow up?' she asked him quickly, with an encouraging smile.

It had the desired effect. He focused again on her, no longer somewhere distant in his mind.

'I grew up in a small Highland village. It's so small I'm not going to bother telling you its name because you'll never have heard of it,' he said jokingly.

'What was it like?' Avril had never been to the North.

'It was home, so I never really thought about it much, but I guess it's a scattering of grey stone cottages surrounded by woodlands and high mountains.'

'It sounds pretty. Do you have brothers and sisters?' She imagined a young Gordon, his fair hair tousled, kicking a ball with several brothers all looking like him.

'No, I'm an only child,' he answered.

The imaginary brothers dissolved into thin air.

'Were *you* lonely?' Avril turned their previous discussion and her confession round on him.

Gordon laughed, and this time it was a good sound. She wished he did so more often. It made his green eyes crinkle nicely at the corners and added a dimple beside his mouth which was somehow alluring. It softened his male jaw, making him at once strong and manly and yet approachable.

'I was never lonely because I had Ronnie. He was my best friend. He was better than a brother. The scrapes and adventures we got into would make your ears burn to listen to. I don't think my parents knew how to handle me, even though I was precious to them. I thought they were elderly, but they can't have been since Father fought in the war with your dad. It was more in their attitude. They were slow to humour — rather dour, in fact. Perhaps that's why I escaped to high jinks with Ronnie.'

'I was surprised to find that Dad knew you,' Avril ventured. 'He never mentioned you or your father before you came here as a lodger.'

'They made a pact during the war. If one of them should fall in battle, the other was to look out for his family. Your dad's been very good to me, writing and keeping in touch and offering me help and support if I needed it. I hadn't taken up any of his offers — until recently when I needed to get away from the Highlands.'

Gordon was quiet. Avril knew by now that he wouldn't tell her why he had to leave.

'So if my Dad hadn't come back from the war but your father had, he would've looked out for my mum,' she mused. 'We might have met that way, too.' It was a fey notion, but it felt as if destiny intended them to meet, whatever the circumstance.

'Yes, we might have,' Gordon agreed.

'So you were a naughty boy,' Avril teased. 'Does that give you an insight into your pupils' behaviour? Do you let them away with nonsense because you used to do it too?'

'I'm a model citizen nowadays,' he said with a smile.

Too much so, in Avril's opinion. It would do him good to loosen up a bit and to relax and have some fun. His tendency to clam up added years to him.

'What about Ronnie? How did he turn out?'

What had she said? Gordon's face was stone.

'Gordon? Did I say something wrong?'

He shook his head, pasting a polite smile on his lips.

'Nothing. It's getting late — I should go upstairs.'

Avril was disappointed. But before Gordon could rise, Linda and David Garnett came in.

'Ah, Avril, there you are,' David wheezed. 'Mum was wondering what you were up to.'

He sat heavily on the sofa. Linda padded softly to sit beside him. She looked weary from the day.

Avril was irked that her mother was still in the habit of keeping tabs on her, but her irritation faded at the sight of Linda's exhaustion.

'Shall I make a pot of tea, Mum?'

'That would be wonderful. Gordon, you'll stay and join us.'

It wasn't a question, it was an expectation. Gordon relaxed back into his seat. When Avril returned with the tea tray, they were all chatting easily. Whatever bad memory she'd triggered in Gordon, it had gone.

She couldn't puzzle him out. She'd discovered tonight that he could be good company. Almost too good. She'd ended up telling him things about herself that no one else knew. But if she infringed on certain topics, he froze up entirely. The problem was that she wasn't sure what the forbidden topics were. All her enquiries had been innocuous enough.

She passed him a cup of tea and their fingertips met briefly. Her skin was hyper-sensitive. She felt each fingertip connect to his, the whorls and patterns momentarily sealed. She looked away, flustered.

Linda looked between them speculatively. Gordon didn't notice but Avril could see that, for once, the frown on her mother's forehead was gone.

The problem was the reason why. *Honestly*, Avril thought with exasperation. If she spent even a few minutes with a man of a suitable age, her mother heard wedding bells.

Angry at that thought, Avril stood up rather abruptly. 'I'm going to say goodnight. I'm tired.'

She was rewarded by two surprised faces and one disappointed one. Her mother would be likely to remain disappointed in the future, if Peggy had her way. Besides, Avril was going out with Jack. And he was one man about whom she knew instinctively that her mother would rather not hear bells.

6

'He's a dreamboat,' Peggy murmured to Avril, watching Gordon count heads as the schoolboys found seats on the railway carriage. Avril had to admit he cut a fine, handsome figure as he stood in the aisle, talking kindly to a child who'd lost his sandwiches. He was drawing admiring glances from women as they boarded the train but was not aware of it one bit.

He couldn't be, with nearly forty children to command. Avril's heart went out to them. They were a motley crew of undersized, skinny boys with white, pinched faces and razored hair. A couple were crying and she saw Peggy move quickly to them and sit to point out of the window at the busy platform scene. Some were over-excited, and one boy had been sick.

By the time the train was on its way,

however, there was some semblance of order. Avril watched out of the window as the tenements and houses flew past, gradually being replaced by grander properties spaced further apart and finally woodland and moors and a wildening sea.

Gordon sat beside her and she felt that surge of unreasonable happiness again.

'This is lovely,' she said happily, meaning the sunny day, the chance to escape the city — and, yes, him sitting beside her.

'Yes,' he agreed and she sensed that he knew exactly what she meant. He grinned and pushed his hat back, making him look momentarily younger and more carefree, then he became serious and responsible again. 'Jimmy's been sick, so I don't think he'll swim. Perhaps it's just as well that I'm staying out of the water.'

'It's a shame about your leg,' Avril ventured, tentatively.

Sure enough, as she had guessed they

would, the shutters came down. He merely grunted, then turned away from her, using the pretence of checking the aisle for stray children.

★　★　★

Avril and Peggy put on their swimsuits in the changing cubicles on the edge of the swimming pool. Avril shivered. It was cool despite the sunny day, and she hoped she'd warm up once she was under the water. There was a great screaming and yelling as the boys plunged into the pool. Peggy had volunteered to help with the non-swimmers in the paddling area, so Avril swam up and down feverishly, getting her muscles moving and looking out for any trouble.

After a while, she relaxed. The boys were too happy to be naughty and thankfully there had been no accidents. She kept catching Gordon's gaze as he sat with Jimmy at the poolside. She gave a little wave which he returned.

All too soon, according to the class's protests, it was time to get changed and move further up the promenade and onto the sandy beach.

'This is the first time some of them have ever been to the seaside,' Gordon explained, as they watched the boys running along the sand.

'That's so sad,' Avril mused. 'We were brought to the seaside as children every year on our holidays. I never thought about how lucky I was.'

'You've got a good heart,' Gordon answered.

It gave her a thrill of pleasure to hear the approval and friendliness in his voice. She wanted his admiration. He sat well back from the sea's edge, against the cement wall of the sloping promenade, and she was reminded of the distaste he had shown for the river.

'You don't like the water, do you?' she asked. 'That's why you didn't swim today. It wasn't your leg at all.'

As she said it, she knew it was true.

For a moment, it seemed that he

wouldn't answer her. Impulsively, she reached for his hand.

The contact stunned them both. She made to pull back, but Gordon squeezed hers more tightly as if drawing strength from her. Reluctantly then, he released her fingers.

'Last year I was involved in a terrible accident. A friend died as a result. My best friend.' He swallowed painfully.

Avril held his hand again, not caring who saw. It felt right.

'You don't need to tell me if you don't want to,' she said quietly. 'It's all right.'

'The car went down an embankment.' Gordon's voice was emotionless, the words stark. 'It fell into a deep river. We were trapped by the pressure on the car doors. I finally got free and I went up for air. By the time I dived down again for Ronnie, it was too late.'

Avril felt the unspeakable horror of it. It was worse, somehow, when told so baldly. Between the words, the unspoken parts of the story rose up as flashing images in her mind. How terrifying it must have been to be trapped in the black water, struggling for breath, the volume of river waters above pressing down on you.

She shivered. Poor, poor Gordon. And yet, in spite of his own suffering, he had tried to save his friend. What solid, stalwart courage that must have required.

'I broke my leg getting free of the car,' he went on. 'But it was nothing compared to how Ronnie must have suffered.'

His jaw was so gripped, Avril could see its sharp angle up to his ear. She longed to soothe its tension away. But it wasn't her place to do so. She could only helplessly pat the back of his hand when she wanted to hug him and hold him and absorb some of the horror from him. Ronnie was the friend he'd spoken so fondly of the other night, describing their childhood pranks.

'You have a fear of water now, which is understandable.'

'I can't stand the sight of it.' Gordon shook his head as though it was mere foolishness on his part. 'It repulses me. I can't help remembering the gloom of the water as the car sank and the taste of it in my mouth as I swam to the surface.'

'You were so brave,' Avril murmured, moved by his distress. 'You tried to save your friend. You did your very best.'

But Gordon's reply was an anguished cry of 'No, no. You don't understand.'

Would he have said more? Avril didn't know, because at that moment Peggy came skidding in the sand towards them.

'What's with the long faces? Come along, it's time for the sandcastle competition.' She grabbed Avril merrily and pulled her up to run along the strand.

Gordon set a schoolmasterly smile on his face and went across to the boys. Peggy ran with Avril along the beach. She felt the soft crunch of the sand loosening beneath her sandals and the heat of the sun burning on the top of her head pleasantly. She grinned at Peggy, whose head was thrown back in sheer delight at the day.

'I feel as if we've escaped school today too,' Avril said.

'We have,' Peggy replied, letting the sun soak in to her skin as she raised her face to it. 'If we weren't here, you'd be cleaning the lodgers' rooms and I'd be tidying up after Mum.' She stopped. 'I should feel guilty for that.'

'You need a break sometimes, Pegs,' Avril said with conviction. 'You're good to your mum. Besides, we can both work extra hard this evening to make up for bunking off now.'

The sea was glittery blue and the lazy waves washed the tide line with swishing movements. The sea seemed to be agreeing with Avril, light-heartedly enticing them to fun.

'You're right,' Peggy cried. 'Look at all this sand. How many sandcastles can we make?'

They reached a huddled group of boys with Gordon in the centre. He was explaining to them how to make a castle out of sand. Avril hadn't thought about that. If it was the first time they'd ever been to the seaside, then it would also be the first time they had ever touched sand or played with it.

'You can mould the sand if it's damp,' Gordon was saying patiently. 'I've brought buckets so you can fill them up from the sea and wet the sand. Any questions?'

A small, thin, mousy-haired boy with a purpling bruise on his shin raised his hand.

'Henry?'

'Please, Sir, my Ma'll kill me if I gets ma shirt wet.'

Gordon was nonplussed. He hesitated, the bucket swinging from his fingers.

Avril heard herself speak. 'Peggy and I can help bring water to anyone who wants some.'

Gordon threw her a grateful glance. 'There we are then. Miss Garnett and Miss Pearson will help you all. Now it's time to get started. Remember to make your castle as imaginative as you can. Decorate it with what you can find on the beach, shells and sticks and feathers. Let's get going.'

The boys scattered, the more confident youngsters immediately finding a patch of beach to work on. A few boys remained, looking uncertain or downright scared.

'Come along with me,' Peggy ordered, leading the little band along the beach. 'We'll find a quiet spot to build on. Avril, can you collect a couple of buckets of sea water, please?'

Avril mock-saluted her friend. Peggy was definitely in charge. She turned back and went over to Gordon to fetch the bucket.

'I wanted to thank you for agreeing to volunteer today,' he said to her.

'I'm enjoying myself,' she said honestly. 'It's like a holiday.'

'I've dreaded it,' Gordon admitted, indicating the sea, which to Avril's eyes looked friendly and inviting. 'But with you here it's more than bearable. And Peggy, too, of course,' he added.

Avril took the bucket from him. 'I'll fill this up, shall I?'

She was surprised when he followed her down to the frothy sea edge. He didn't offer to fill the bucket and his back was rigid, but he was there.

'It wouldn't do the boys any good to see me fearful of the water,' he explained.

They walked back companionably to where Peggy had arranged a smoothed-out circle of sand and was demonstrating the art of making a sandcastle to her timid little group.

Avril poured a little water, darkening the sand. Gordon began to dig it with the trowel he'd brought. He patted it into the bucket and turned it over. He tapped it hard with the back of the trowel and everyone held their breath as he slid the bucket up. There was a perfect tower of sand. The boys clapped spontaneously.

Gordon grinned happily. 'That's how it's done. Right, Henry, here's a bucket. Tommy, you take the other. Lewis and Graeme can be in charge of the trowels. See if you can all make a tower and then decorate it with cockles.'

He knelt to help Henry, oblivious to the fact that his trouser knees were stained with damp sand.

He was more relaxed than she'd seen him, Avril thought. He was a good teacher and the boys obviously adored him. Whatever kept him closed in normally disappeared when he was teaching.

He had been terribly affected by what happened to him and Ronnie; that was clear. What had he meant when he told her she didn't understand? She watched him talking to the boys quietly and in a kindly fashion, his fair hair ruffled in the odd little breeze from the sea.

She tried to imagine losing Peggy. It

would be awful, and it would leave her very lonely. She, too, would have attempted to fill that space with work. But at least she had a large family to turn to. Her parents were neither old nor dour. And she had a brother and sisters, while Gordon had none. Yet she wondered why he'd decided to uproot himself from his village home. What had he said, the other night, as they chatted in front of the fire? *I needed to get away from the Highlands.* His parents were both dead. He had no ties to keep him there. But he'd implied he was escaping from something. Or someone.

'Miss Garnett will help you with that, Tommy,' Gordon said, turning easily to Avril.

She saw the boy struggling to lift a bucket overflowing with a sodden sludge of sand. Gordon was busy sticking feathers onto another creation. She took the heavy bucket and turned it fast. It stuck to the ground with a thud.

'Now give it a bash with the trowel,'

she told the boy.

Tommy whacked it good and proper, several times for good measure. Avril lifted the bucket and a gluey tower appeared. The boys cheered.

Avril looked for Gordon. He was being led away by some boys to admire their competition entries, but he met her gaze. There was something in his expression which made her catch her breath. Then he looked away with a half-smile and it was gone.

She watched him walk away across the drifts of shells and weed. *We could be friends*. It rushed into her head. She would make sure he wasn't lonely any more.

'Isn't this fun!' Peggy whooped. The boys nearby cheered. Her happiness was infectious. She shoved up sand to make castle ramparts for a small sickly-looking boy with thick, smudged spectacles.

'You're a natural with the children,' Avril remarked. 'I don't believe I've ever seen you so content.'

'I'm really enjoying myself,' Peggy confessed. She had a swipe of sand on her cheek but evidently didn't care. 'I could become a school teacher. Maybe I should.' She sat quite still, taken with this novel idea.

'It would stop you getting bored, certainly.' Avril laughed. 'But you wouldn't be able to get married.'

Peggy stopped digging and stared at her. 'Why ever not?'

'I'm not sure, but I think once you're married you'd have to give up your job to stay at home and look after your husband.'

Peggy stared ruefully along the beach to where Gordon was hunkered, putting shells on a particularly fine sandcastle.

'What a pity.'

Avril's mind was buzzing with Gordon's confession. He was wounded physically and emotionally by the accident; it explained in part why he was closed off. He must dwell on it — relive it. She resolved to be as good a friend as she could to him.

She was tired all of a sudden, from the journey and the swimming, but curiously contented. There were diamond coruscations on the waves, a sweet breeze and the sand was crunchy and tepid under her toes. She'd slipped off her sandals to burrow her feet into the beach. She grabbed her bag and found her notebook. It would be great to try to capture the marvellous day in a few descriptive lines.

Away along the beach now, Peggy was jostling Gordon and she heard her friend's loud laughter. The boys were crowding round them, shouting about the sandcastles. The competition judging was underway. She had some glorious minutes to spend writing, getting the imagery right and immortalising her emotions if she could.

*   *   *

She was so absorbed in her writing that she didn't notice Gordon until he was right beside her.

'What's this? Noting the prize winners? Donald and Jimmy had to share the top prize in the end. Both brilliant.' He spoke heartily and Avril guessed that he wanted to forget their conversation earlier about the accident and Ronnie. She went along with it, although the more she dwelt on it, the more she wanted to find out how it had affected him.

'What was the prize? Escaping homework for a week?'

'Not quite as good as that. Ice creams. Quite a treat for this lot. What are you writing?' He sounded genuinely interested.

'It's nothing,' Avril said hastily, stashing her notebook. It was a knee-jerk reaction. She kept it hidden from the world.

'I don't believe it's nothing,' Gordon said gently. 'Is it a hobby of yours?'

'I like to write. In fact I've written some stories. I even sold one to a women's magazine.' Avril kicked up sand and watched the miniature crystals spray onto the stones. 'Don't tell my mother that,' she added hurriedly. It was her secret, one that Mum would think highly un-ladylike. Selling a story!

'I'm not on such familiar terms with your mother, to be able to confide such things,' Gordon said ironically. 'Your secret's safe with me.'

And yours with me. She didn't say it, but their gazes locked and she didn't have to.

On impulse, she thrust the notebook at him. Gordon took it. He bent his head to concentrate on it. She had a crazy impulse to run her hand through his thick hair. To feel the softness of it and the warmth of his neck where the sun licked it.

'This is wonderful. You've captured the day most poetically,' he said with admiration.

Avril took the papers back. She had laid herself bare on the page; that was why she never shared her writing

121

with anyone. It gave too much of her away. She should be embarrassed now that Gordon had read her innermost thoughts. But, strangely, she wasn't — they would be safe with him.

'Do you ever write?' she asked. It came to her that it might help him as it did her. Anger, frustrations even sorrow vanished or was ameliorated by transmitting it in ink to the paper. 'It could help you think things through. You could write about Ronnie . . .'

But she'd pushed too far.

'It's time to go,' Gordon said brusquely. He stood up.

'Right.' Avril scrambled to her feet and brushed off the sand.

Gordon paused. 'It's been fun. Thank you.'

It was an apology of sorts, she felt. It was all she would get out of him in any case, for the spell was broken. She wished she hadn't mentioned Ronnie; it was too painful to him.

Avril sighed. It had been lovely today but just as she felt she was getting to know him, Gordon had pushed her away.

She went to find Peggy, who was wiping the remains of an ice-cream from her mouth and promised to fetch Avril one to take along on their journey back to the railway station. The boys were tired but content and there was no squabbling, just friendly argument over whose sandcastle had really been the best.

* * *

Gordon tramped along the beach, feeling a familiar painful twinge in his hip. It served him right. Avril Garnett was getting right under his skin. There was something about her.

He cursed himself. He should never have told her about the accident and Ronnie! She made it too easy to talk to her. He felt again the satin touch of her skin on his. She offered comfort, but his body wanted more — even in his distress, desire had flooded him. He should keep away from her.

But he knew he wouldn't, even if it could only lead to heartache. If she knew the truth about him, she would run a mile, he was convinced of it. He was not what she thought he was. He was a sham. Worse than that; he was a murderer.

7

'Gloria's missing. You have to do something! Avril, wake up.' Shirley's frantic voice penetrated Avril's foggy head. She came to slowly, wondering what was going on. She was lying on her bed, her head on a hard pillow. She focussed in on it fuzzily; it was her open notebook. She must have dozed off while writing. It was still light outside, but it was the beautiful aquamarine shade that heralds the evening and promises a star soon.

'Why are you sleeping?' Shirley cried. 'You need to get up.'

'Okay,' Avril mumbled. She swung her legs down over the side of the bed and rubbed her eyes. Her hair had come out of its ponytail and hung loose to her shoulders.

'Did you hear me? Gloria's gone. We have to go and get her.'

'Slow down,' Avril mumbled. 'Tell me what you mean.' She patted the bed and Shirley thumped down onto it, twisting a lock of hair round and round her finger in agitation.

'She must've sneaked out to see Helen. Why didn't she tell me? Why didn't she take me with her?' Shirley burst into tears.

'You're not making any sense,' Avril said sharply. She resisted the urge to shake Shirley. Suddenly she was wide awake and on edge. If Gloria was really missing, that was serious. 'Who's Helen?'

'She's a girl we met on the trams.' Shirley sniffled. 'Gloria and I were going into town one day a few weeks ago and we saw this girl. She wasn't dressed very well but she was friendly and we got chatting. Then we kept bumping into her on the tram. She was playing a game on them, trying to avoid the conductor — I don't think she paid a single ticket.' Shirley paused with admiration. 'Anyway, she invited us to

126

go and visit her home. Of course we said no. But I think Gloria's gone there today.'

'Was Helen the reason Gloria didn't go to the knitting bee?' Avril asked.

Shirley nodded. 'She asked me to cover for her. She was meeting Helen in the city centre. She knew Mum wouldn't approve of Helen. She . . . she smells funny, and her hair needs brushing.'

Avril could quite believe that those attributes would condemn the girl in her mother's respectable eyes.

'But Gloria's become friendly with Helen, just the same.'

Or probably because of her mother's attitudes, Avril reflected; Gloria could be stubborn. Thrawn, even.

'Helen's a lot of fun. And she's different from our other friends,' Shirley said, wiping her nose on her sleeve. 'What are we going to do? If Mum finds out that Gloria's sneaked out, she'll be mad.'

'We'll have to make sure she doesn't

find out, then,' Avril retorted. 'We have to get Gloria back before dinner time. Which gives us a couple of hours.' She thought quickly. 'Do you know where the girl lives?'

Shirley nodded again. 'We passed it on the tram and she pointed out her building. I can't remember the street name but I can lead us there.'

'Right,' Avril said, a surge of excitement and adventure leaping up in her. 'Go and get your coat on. Gordon will help us, I'm sure. I'll go and ask him to come with us.'

She didn't fancy searching the slums as dark crept in. But with Gordon it would be absolutely fine.

Shirley ran off and Avril went to knock on Gordon's door.

He was sitting at his desk, a great stack of jotters towering beside him. His face brightened at the sight of her.

'Hello. Come in, Avril. I could use an excuse to break from marking this lot. You wouldn't believe the many different ways the boys can spell. They're very inventive — so much so, I've lost faith in my own spelling. What's the matter?' he finished, noticing then the urgency in her stance.

'Gloria's missing. Shirley thinks she's visiting a girl in the East End. Would you come with us to fetch her home, please?'

'Of course.' Gordon wasted no time in questions, but threw on his trench coat and followed Avril downstairs where Shirley was waiting at the door impatiently.

Avril filled him in on the details as they caught a tram heading east to the city centre and beyond. They were about to venture into parts of the city Avril had never been to, had never had reason to go to. She felt a great sense of anticipation and exploration, her adrenaline running high and on full alert. Beside her, Shirley nibbled on her fingernails, staring out of the tram and across the busy street.

Cars drove alongside, some danger-ously close to the tram while pedestrians dashed in front of it carelessly, confident of making it across the street without incident. There were streams of late shoppers in and out of the doorways under the colourful awnings, desperate to make their last purchases before the shops shut for the night. Some of the shop keepers were already pulling down the shutters, using great metal hooked poles. Others were mopping and swilling out pails of frothy grey water onto the pavements and down into the drains. An ancient Clydesdale horse stood by the fruit seller's stall, its head down resting as the stallholder packed empty wooden boxes onto the overflowing cart the poor beast would soon be required to pull.

Avril was glad of Gordon sitting next to her on the battered leather seats. The bump and sway of the tram pushed her against him but it felt good and familiar, even as she apologised.

The ordered chaos of the main shopping streets soon gave way to narrower, grimier roads. The majestic buildings became gapped, blackened tenement blocks like rotten teeth in the skyline. They had changed trams at Charing Cross.

Shirley leaned forward intently. Suddenly she pointed. 'That's it! Over there. That's the street Helen lives on.'

They found themselves on a dirty side street as the tram rumbled away taking its bubble of familiarity and security with it. Avril was intensely glad of Gordon's presence. It was an alien part of the city. The tenements were in a poor state of repair. One building had crumbled altogether and a wall had fallen off, exposing a column of rooms and fireplaces, now hanging precariously in the open air. Other buildings were still inhabited despite broken windows, and everywhere there was a layer of soot and grime. The very air was laden with a veil of fog, courtesy of nearby factory chimneys billowing out clouds of fumes. Avril stood uncertainly.

'What will we do?' she asked Gordon. 'We can't simply barge into Helen's

131

home after Gloria.'

'We can ask around,' Gordon suggested, indicating the many children scattered on the pavements, embroiled in games. 'Gloria and Helen may well be playing outside in a back court.'

As they discussed this, a smartly dressed woman on a bicycle whizzed by and came to a halt. She was entirely dressed in green, from her belted trench coat to her buttoned-up dress and hat.

'It's the green lady,' Shirley piped up. 'We could ask her.'

'Great idea,' Gordon told her warmly.

The green ladies, as the health visitors were known due to their uniform, knew the back courts and narrow lanes well. Miss Dale was no exception.

'Helen? Let me see. That's probably Helen MacRae. I was in seeing her mother last year with the new baby — child number ten it was, the poor woman. Still, she's lucky to have a doting husband. Very unusual to find that, I can tell you.'

She gave Gordon a severe look. Avril's impulse was to deny he was her husband. She bit her lip. Gordon's lips twitched in amusement. He was clearly enjoying himself. It struck her then that perhaps he needed a bit of excitement in his life, too.

Miss Dale directed them, in a clear, piercing voice, to the MacRae's single end dwelling, as she called it. Shirley hung back, intimidated by both Miss Dale's briskness and her surroundings. Avril, boosted by her adventure, took Shirley's hand comfortingly and they went forward with Gordon's tall frame behind them.

They entered a gloomy close which stank of damp brick and neglect. Narrow, steep steps led up and off to various homes. A gaggle of little boys ran past them to the outside.

Helen's home was on the top floor. Avril wondered how Gloria had the courage to come to this place all by herself. How could people live like this? It was depressing and bleak.

'They've no choice,' Gordon said, answering the despair he saw in her face. Then she was embarrassed and angry at herself. Of course they didn't have a choice. They couldn't just up and move. They were stuck here forever.

A little flame ignited within her and started to burn. It was a sense of injustice in the world.

* * *

'Helen?' The girl who opened the door was shorter than the twins and stick-thin with dirty blonde hair. Avril started to explain who she was, when Gloria's head appeared behind Helen. Her eyes were bright with indignation.

'Have you seen the state of the stairs?' was her greeting. 'Can you believe that Helen and her family have to live in only two rooms? There's twelve of them. It's appalling. We have to do something about it.'

Helen stared at them all in turn, not

bothered by Gloria's dramatic outburst or by their appearance on her doorstep.

She grinned at Shirley, showing yellow, uneven teeth. 'Ma's oot. You coming to play?'

'Perhaps another day,' Avril said kindly. 'We've come to get Gloria. It's nearly dinner time.'

Helen backed away into the house and Avril went in, unthinkingly. Behind her, Gordon held Shirley back and they stood waiting on the doorstep, which was probably best.

The room was small and stuffy. There was a box bed built into the far wall and a mattress upturned on its side leaning against the wall. A table with the remains of a meal on it stood centre in the room. Through another door, Avril glimpsed a cooking range, pots and pans.

She was horrified. How could twelve people live in a space this size? Where did they all sleep? A wash of shame hit her like a tsunami and she staggered to sit on the one chair in the room. She had set out to get Gloria as if on a journey of exploration, naively happy and thrilled to be going to the East End. She had used Helen's situation as a titillation because she was bored with her own life.

But this was real. It wasn't a side entertainment for her, to take her mind off the humdrum days at the boarding house. She and Gloria could walk away from this, but Helen couldn't.

'It's awful, Avril. People shouldn't live like this,' Gloria said passionately. Her blue eyes were damp.

'I know,' Avril said helplessly. She was conscious of Helen watching them curiously. 'Come along, Gloria, get your coat. We have to go.'

For a moment she thought Gloria might refuse. She looked fiercely at her older sibling, and Avril realised her little sister was growing up. Gloria was maturing in personality. She was no longer the little girl obsessed only with sweets and fashions. Helen's friendship had opened her eyes to another world.

And mine, too, she conceded. *I'll never be the same after seeing this.*

Gordon and Shirley had gone down to stand in the street. Avril turned to chivvy Gloria into speeding up when a young woman, about her own age, appeared in the doorway. She had her hands on her hips aggressively and her face was hard.

'Who are you? What are you doing here in our hoose? Dogooders, are ye? Out! Out!'

'Agnes, it's ma friend Gloria,' Helen wailed. 'Leave her be.'

But Agnes' mouth was set in a grim line and she advanced menacingly. Avril quickly set herself between the angry young woman and Gloria.

'We're just leaving, thank you,' she said calmly. 'Gloria's had a lovely time with Helen. We don't want any trouble.'

'Trouble? I could knock you down wi' nae trouble,' Agnes sneered.

Avril's chest tightened and her pulse rattled like a runaway steam engine. But she tilted her chin and held her

ground. 'There's no need for unpleas-
antness. We're leaving. Goodbye, Helen
— thank you for inviting Gloria round.'

'She didn't exactly . . . ' Gloria
started, then stopped as Avril squeezed
her arm hard.

Obediently, she stepped behind Avril
and they did a strange foxtrot to the
door, Avril always a barrier between her
sister and Agnes. The young woman
guffawed. She let them go.

As they ran the last few steps down to
reach Gordon, Agnes flung up the
tenement window to shout down, 'And
don't come back! Your sort isn't wanted
around here. Snobs.'

★   ★   ★

The boarding house was peaceful. Mrs
Garnett had gone out to the neighbours to discuss the Coronation party,
Mrs Petrocelli told Avril when they
returned. The old lady hoped dinner
wouldn't be too delayed, and Avril
tried to reassure her it wouldn't be.

She made a pot of tea and took it in to the sitting room to find Gordon. Gloria and Shirley had been sent upstairs to wash and tidy up before their mother returned.

'I had no idea people lived like that,' Avril murmured.

'The housing is improving but it's taking a shockingly long time,' Gordon agreed. 'Some of my pupils live near Helen in similar circumstances, but I've lost others whose families have moved out to new housing with plenty of bedrooms and indoor plumbing.' He paused, regarding her. 'What is it?'

'It's me,' she confessed honestly. 'I went there today out of concern for Gloria, yes. But also out of a sense of adventure, of fun. It was so wrong of me. When I saw the surroundings, like Gloria, I was angry. But what can I do? I can't change it.'

Gordon drank his tea. He stood and paced, his limp more pronounced after the journey on the trams.

'You could write about it,' he said.

'There's power in the written word. The more people know about it, the more inclined they will be to help and to make changes.'

'Could I?' Avril wondered aloud. It was a different matter from writing stories.

'Why not?' he urged. 'At least give it a go.'

Avril stood in agitation, her mind swirling with possibilities. It was a terrifying, fantastic suggestion. She was standing close to him, lost in imagination. She looked up and smiled. His eyes were so very green, like the depths of a pool in the Highland glens. Avril leaned in instinctively, her lips parted. Gordon murmured her name. The air crackled between them, alive.

Gloria and Shirley came slamming down the stairs and burst into the living room, both chattering at once. Gordon limped to the chair and Avril poured more tea. Then the front door opened and Avril heard her mother's sigh. She was home, and it was dinner time at the boarding house. The moment was lost.

As she served up chicken pie and potatoes, Avril wondered what had happened. Was he going to kiss her? Did she want him to? Would she have let him? She brushed it away.

But one thought kept coming back to her. In the instant of crisis, when Gloria was missing, it was Gordon to whom she'd turned for help without thinking.

★   ★   ★

He would have kissed her. Gordon stared at the jotters. With a sigh of exasperation he pushed them aside. He couldn't concentrate. All he could see was Avril's face tilted up to his. The chemistry between them was undeniable. He could almost taste the sweetness of her lips under his. As if in a spell, he'd been drawn to her. The interruption by the twins had stopped him. Which he was glad of, he told himself. He didn't know what Avril's reaction would have been.

The problem was, he couldn't help himself. The fact was, he was falling in love with her. It was no longer simply a deep physical attraction alone. She was intelligent and lively and fun to be with, and she had a kind and loving heart. Her compassion today at the slums and her driving need to change things for the better had touched him. Like a tumbler of locks in a keyhole, his heart had been irretrievably moved.

Gordon felt himself thawing. His self-imposed restraint was loosening and there was a fleck of light in the future. He picked up his jacket. It was dark now, but it needn't stop him. He would force himself to face the river. A ripple of unease tickled his spine, but he ignored it. Gloria had described how bravely Avril had faced down Helen's sister and protected her. If Avril could show bravery, surely he could too. It would be a relief not to live in the shadows of fear any longer. He would work on his water phobia and vanquish it.

He slipped Lucille's latest letter into his pocket to read on his walk and headed downstairs, intending to make for Avril's secret stream and the riverside walkway. There was a man lounging in the hallway talking to Davey; Gordon recognised him. It was the fellow who'd been walking with Avril at the weekend. He had a cockiness about him that Gordon disliked. But Avril, arriving from the dining room and greeting him, seemed oblivious. More than that, she obviously liked him.

Gordon acknowledged the group stiffly and went outside, pretending not to hear Avril's call to him. He didn't expect anything from his love for her. He had no intention of declaring it. It would warm him, that was all. He was still the same man with the same guilt.

He steeled himself at the sound of the water lapping against the bank. In the darkness, the river took on a kind of beauty. It was impossible to see the debris and the chemical oils that covered its surface. Instead, a kindly moon cast its silvery tracks onto the water and the city lights twinkled star-like in its reflections. He took one heavy step and then another. A nausea rose up in his throat but he swallowed it down. *I can do this*, he promised himself.

He came at last to the water's edge, keeping his image of Avril's face in front of him as comfort and guide.

'Yes,' Gordon said to the river, 'I'm here. I'll be back every day from now on, until I've beaten you.'

The water lapped noisily in answer.

Strangely at peace, Gordon drew Lucille's letter out and tore it open. Maybe, just maybe, this one would be different. But as he read it, the words pulled him like sucking whirlpools once more into the past.

★   ★   ★

Jack was upbeat. He'd had the brilliant idea of coming to visit Davey so he could meet up with Avril. Just the sight of her neat figure and pretty face was enough to heat him up. He wanted her more each time he saw her. Funny how the other girls left him cold. He had a few casual girlfriends always ready to go out on a date. But lately he hadn't called them and when they called him, he hadn't answered. He was desperate for only one girl, and that was Avril Garnett.

'Avril, you look charming this evening.' He cut rudely over Davey's tedious conversation about a broken guitar string. Davey looked offended but Jack didn't care.

'Jack,' she said nicely. At that moment, a chap about his own age came down the stairs. He was nothing special, Jack reckoned, especially with that limp. So he was mildly annoyed when Avril favoured him with a gorgeous smile. Jack was relieved when the fellow barely said hello back and disappeared out the door. There was no love lost there, then, he was glad to see.

He jumped past Davey so he was standing next to Avril, his coat brushing her legs. He itched to let his hands do likewise.

'I was worried about you,' Avril was saying. 'Those men last week. You never did explain what they wanted with you.'

And he had no intention of doing so now. Avril was far too prim and proper to hear the full story. Jack suspected she wouldn't understand the predicament he'd found himself in. Luckily he had come to an amicable agreement with Shorty and his sidekick. He'd paid back some of the money, with the promise of the rest very, very soon. He was confident he'd make the money in time. So he waved her concerns away.

Davey slunk off, which was gratifying.

'You should've seen it, Jack. It was truly awful living conditions. That poor child and her family.' He'd missed the beginning of what Avril was saying, caught up in his thoughts on Shorty. He nodded as if agreeing, wondering what she was talking about.

'What would you do in the circumstances?' Avril asked, her dark eyes sad, as she waited for his answer.

'Poor people?' He said, catching the gist of it. 'There's plenty of them. Always will be, come to that. Nothing you can do. Besides — ' he winked — 'they're not that badly off. I've sold a lot of stuff down that end of town.' There were a lot of gullible people about at both ends of town — and the middle part too.

Avril looked disappointed in him, so Jack searched for a change of topic. 'You and Peggy still coming dancing with me on Saturday?'

'Oh — I'd forgotten about that,' Avril admitted. 'Yes — I'd like to, I think.'

Forgotten. She didn't sound too enthusiastic either. Jack's confidence slipped a notch. Still, wait until he had her with him in the confines of the dance hall he'd chosen. It would be wall to wall bodies, no chance to squeeze away. He could barely wait. Once he'd had an opportunity to kiss her, Avril would soon change her tune. She'd be smitten with him. No doubt about that — it would be all change on Saturday night.

8

Avril's hand was cramped. Her pencil fairly flew backwards and forwards on the page as she tried to set down her feelings and descriptions of the slums. She was so absorbed in her task that she barely heard Peggy's cheerful hello. With a start, she looked up.

'Is it time to get ready so soon?' she gasped.

Peggy laughed. She was carrying a bulging bag full of her party clothes and make-up which she dumped on the floor. 'It doesn't feel like that to me. I've been waiting all day to get ready for the dancing tonight. It's going to be marvellous. Now budge over and let's get our nails painted. I've brought shell-pink, pearly white or clear varnish. What do you want?'

Avril wasn't sure what she wanted. It was strange that a couple of weeks ago she'd been dying to go dancing with Jack. And now . . . well, her writing was so all-consuming that she'd be just as happy staying in to complete her article. Happier, in fact. It was compulsive and interesting and she really wanted to finish it, polish it up and show it to Gordon. He was a school teacher after all, she rationalised, so he could correct her spelling and grammar. Besides, he was genuinely interested in her project and she could share it with no one else. Her mother would be scandalised, her father was too absent at his allotment, Davey would switch off once he saw it had nothing to do with music, and the twins were too young.

'Avril? You don't look too excited. What's the matter? You still want to dance, don't you? Jack's keen on you. Tonight might be the night.' Peggy nudged her with a grin.

'I don't know what the matter is with me.' Avril sighed. 'I think I want to go dancing, but I'm not as excited as I thought I'd be. I'm being silly.'

'We'll get in the mood while we dress,' Peggy promised. 'What about Jack? You still like him, don't you?'

She did, didn't she? He was dashing and attractive and charming. He was attentive, too. Okay, he'd disappointed her with his lukewarm view on the suffering in the slums, but perhaps she was expecting too much from him. Not everyone would be interested in it. Besides, Jack hadn't seen what she had. She was being too hard on him.

'Yes, I do like Jack,' Avril said firmly. 'Don't mind me, Peggy. I'm in a funny mood, is all.'

'Well buck out of it,' Peggy said cheekily. 'Here, what do you think of my new dress?'

★　★　★

An hour later they were almost ready. Peggy had painted their nails and they'd styled their hair. Avril wore a white, short-sleeved top she'd borrowed

151

from Peggy. It was tight-fitting in all the right places and showed off her slim waist. She matched it with a full navy-blue skirt and petticoats. The skirt swished satisfyingly when she walked and flew out when she spun round.

Peggy clapped her hands and let out a peal of laughter.

'It's perfect. You look amazing. Now what about me?'

Avril pretended to scrutinise her friend, narrowing her eyes critically and walking around her. Peggy's new dress was pastel green. It was long and narrow with a generous pleat at the back so she could move easily on the dance floor.

'You look great,' she announced. 'Now, let's pick up our handbags and slip on our shoes. Where are we meeting Jack?'

'Over at my home. I thought it best. We don't want your mum asking too many questions, do we? This way she'll think you're going to the Locarno as usual.'

Avril felt a twinge of guilt; it wasn't fair to deceive her mother. On the other hand, if she knew where they were going, she would definitely forbid them. Besides, she wasn't lying to her. What she didn't know wouldn't hurt her. Avril would be back at the usual hour because she'd make sure Jack got her home punctually, and everything would be fine.

'Let's go,' she said. 'I'm looking forward to it now.'

She loved dancing. It was going to be all right.

They stepped next door and found Jack waiting in the shadows. He looked darkly attractive in a velvet-collared jacket and charcoal trousers with his trademark shined shoes. His hair was slicked back and his eyes glittered when he saw Avril.

'I'm a lucky man to walk out with two such beautiful ladies,' he declared gallantly, offering an arm to each of them. 'It's the tram tonight, girls, the car's in the garage.'

They travelled east, further than Avril had been before. She recognised Helen's part of town, but even it went past. The tram stopped beside a jostling queue of people on the pavement and Avril was confused when Jack joined it.

'We wait here to get into the dance hall,' he explained, grinning at her astonishment.

'It's very popular,' she said, suddenly glad of Peggy beside her. The crowd was good-humoured and raucous, but it wasn't the kind of crowd she was used to. Their usual dance hall was much more sedate, with girls like themselves and young men who were well groomed, like Davey or Gordon.

Gordon. Avril wished he was with her. For some reason, he gave her security and confidence. Her tummy was full of butterfly nerves. The girls in front of them were screeching over to an older man on the street corner, their lips vividly painted and their tops shockingly low-cut. The man leered back and shouted something indecipherable in a thick accent.

Peggy squeezed her hand and winked. Her face was lit up with excitement. Avril's nerves intensified in a flash; Peggy wasn't worried, and she was alone in feeling vulnerable.

She took a deep breath and then another. She was being daft. She was perfectly safe. She had Jack on one side of her and Peggy on the other. So why did she still desperately wish for Gordon to be here?

She conjured up his face for comfort and resolve. It was a handsome face, with a strong jaw and those extraordinary eyes. His fair hair was so short. She tried to imagine it longer, swept back in a style like Jack's, and failed. Gordon was fine the way he was; she didn't need to change him.

The queue was moving now, surging forward. She stumbled and would have fallen but for Jack's strong grip.

'They're opening the doors.' He

grinned. 'There's usually a bit of a cram to get in. Don't worry, I've got you.'

Somehow they pushed their way through the bottleneck at the door and burst into the dance hall. Avril's nostrils were full of the smells of cheap perfume and body sweat and cigarettes. Someone had jabbed her side with a sharp elbow and a girl's heel had gone painfully onto to the top of her foot. She was battered and bruised, and the dancing hadn't even begun!

Jack manoeuvred them over to a table, and she sank down gratefully and looked around. The dance floor was enormous, a great sheet of polished wooden planks. At the far end on a raised platform was the dance band. They weren't playing yet but were laughing and chatting to each other as they tuned their instruments and adjusted music and stands. There was a long counter along the length of one wall where drinks and snacks could be purchased. Jack was leaning on it casually, chatting to the man next to him. Avril envied him his relaxed aura. Beside her, Peggy was anything but relaxed. She kept giving little screams and pointing people out to Avril.

'Do you think we use dance cards here?' Avril asked her.

'Doesn't look like it.' Peggy stared about her. 'Just remember it's rude to refuse to dance if someone asks you. If you don't get up with them, you'd better sit that dance out.'

Jack came back, whistling, and put down three drinks.

'What's this?' Avril said cautiously. 'Is it orange juice?'

'Special orange juice,' Jack agreed, a little too heartily.

Before she could ask him to explain what he meant, the band started up with an overly loud trumpeting. With a great roar of approval, people swarmed onto the dance floor for the first number. Jack grabbed Avril and spun her out onto the floor. She felt her skirt billow out prettily and her spirits lifted. She would enjoy herself. It was mean of her not to, when Jack had gone to the bother of escorting them here. He was in his element and she would join in.

The first dance was a fast waltz, and she was good at dancing. Avril's feet quickly found the rhythm and she wheeled round, following Jack's lead. She glimpsed Peggy in the arms of a tall, thin man, her mouth open in laughter. Avril relaxed into the music and started to feel good. At the end of the dance she twirled happily back to her seat. She was very thirsty, it was such a hot room. She drank the orange juice. It had a funny aftertaste but it quenched her thirst and she asked Jack for another.

The band began the music for a quickstep.

'Oh, I love that,' she cried to herself and leapt up. A man smiled and came towards her but Jack nimbly stepped in to claim the dance. They moved about over the dance floor with ease. Avril gazed around, eager to experience it all.

She recognised a face in the crowd,

but couldn't place it immediately. Then she realised it was Agnes — the woman from the tenement. She was all done up for a Saturday night out, which was why Avril had taken a minute or two to name her. Her straggly blonde hair was pulled back into a clasp and she had powder and eyeshadow on, making her look older. She wore a navy-blue skirt not unlike Avril's own, and she was dancing with a short, chubby man whose head barely reached her shoulder. Avril wondered if Agnes had seen her and recognised her. She fervently hoped not. A memory of Agnes shouting down at them from the top window made her shudder.

However the dance hall was large, and busy. With any luck she needn't bump into Agnes at all.

'I need a rest,' she shouted to Jack. He steered her expertly round another couple and brought her back to the table.

'I'll get more drinks,' he said and went off, winding through the bodies in the direction of the counter.

Peggy flung herself down beside Avril, panting. Her hair curled damply from her forehead and she fanned herself. 'Gosh, it's hot in here. I'm melting. Are you having fun yet?'

'Yes, I am,' Avril said, and meant it.

Peggy leaned forward so that she could speak and be heard without shouting.

'I asked Gordon to come with me tonight, you know.'

'You did what?'

Peggy shrugged, a little bit embarrassed. 'Hey, it's 1953, not the Dark Ages. A girl ought to be able to ask a chap out.'

Privately Avril thought it was a bit forward of Peggy, but she didn't say that. 'What did he say?'

'He's not here, is he? So that gives the game away,' Peggy returned wryly. She took a swig of her drink and made a face. 'What is this stuff?'

But Avril was more interested in what Gordon's reaction to Peggy's invitation was. 'Does he not dance? I suppose his leg wouldn't allow him to.'

'That was his excuse — but he wouldn't have come with me anyway,' Peggy declared.

'That's a bit harsh. He's probably the old-fashioned kind of man who prefers to do the asking. Be patient, Pegs, and he may well ask you out.'

'You and I both know that's not going to happen,' Peggy said, looking at Avril strangely.

'Why ever not?' Avril was flustered. Peggy was right, it was very hot in the dance hall.

'Are you blind? It's obvious Gordon likes you. What's your secret, Avril? It's not enough that you've got Jack panting after you. You've got to steal a perfect man like Gordon, too.'

Peggy's tone was jovial but there was a bitter edge to it.

Avril started to answer but Peggy pretended not to notice and allowed herself to be swept up by a large, beefy man onto the floor for a foxtrot.

Avril sat still in the middle of the noisy chaos. Peggy was wrong. Gordon didn't like her in that way. They were becoming friends, that was true. But she'd relived the strange moment between them in the living room, over and over, and had concluded that she'd imagined it. He hadn't been going to kiss her at all. Why she'd ever thought so was beyond her now.

In this frame of mind, she found Jack's gaze upon her.

'It's boiling in here. Fancy a breath of fresh air?'

'Great idea,' she answered gratefully. It would be good to escape the clamour for a little while. Also good to get a break from Peggy, she thought. She followed Jack out of a side door which led into a cobbled alley. It wasn't the most salubrious of places; there were great scattered stacks of old boxes dumped there and the ground was littered with cigarette butts. A rangy black cat walked delicately along the top of a high brick wall. However, the air was blessedly cool and gentle on her flushed skin. Avril took a big breath of it.

Jack shuffled his feet and gave a little cough. She smiled up at him. She was having a good time tonight.

'Avril, you are beautiful. Can I kiss you?' The words tumbled from Jack's lips.

He looked unsure of himself, which she found endearing. She was curious, too. What would it feel like? He was a good-looking man and she liked him. Being asked straight out like that was unnerving and she'd always imagined she'd be swept off her feet. But she nodded, caught up in the thrill and strangeness of the evening.

Jack leaned in and pressed his lips to hers. She waited, hopefully. Shouldn't she feel more? Weren't there supposed to be violins and stars and magic all at once? She kissed him back but there were no fireworks.

Jack was pleased with it, she could tell. Perhaps it was just her. She had nothing to compare it with, except what was offered in films, and they were most likely exaggerated.

'Shall we go back in now? I'm rather cold,' she said lamely.

★ ★ ★

It was, if anything, even noisier in the hall than when they'd gone outside.

'Oh, there you are. I was getting worried,' Peggy cried. 'Where were you?' She hugged Avril hard and Avril knew she'd been forgiven and that all was well between them once more.

She sipped her drink and grimaced. There was an odd flavour to it and her head was getting fuzzy. She refused another dance, content to sit and watch as Jack pulled Peggy round the dance floor exuberantly.

The back of her head prickled with the sense that someone was staring at her. She turned to see Agnes looking right at her from the other side of the room. Emboldened by the atmosphere,

164

Avril stared right back at her. The young woman twisted her lips into a faint sneer and deliberately turned to her companion, ignoring Avril.

Avril cast about, noting fashions which worked well and some which were ghastly. She became aware of groups of men on either side of the dance floor. They weren't dancing and they weren't talking. That's what marked them out from the rest of the groups. They stood still, watching each other across the dancing couples. With horror, Avril noticed the two men who had accosted Jack in the coffee bar. There was no mistaking them. There was the beanpole man with the missing front teeth, and beside him his friend who reminded her of a toad. He was even wearing the same revolting striped suit.

Before she could react, the crowds on both sides swelled like waves on the ocean, intent on crashing into each other. A woman screamed and people fled the floor as the gangs of men met and clashed right there on the polished wood. A great roar rose up to the ceiling and in the mayhem Avril was convinced she saw the flash of a metal blade. Then she was being pulled along by a surge of frightened girls.

'Jack! Peggy!' she yelled. She could see Peggy's blonde cropped hair but she was being taken in the other direction by her dance partner, the beefy man from earlier. Avril searched desperately for Jack in the melée. She cried out as her hair caught in a girl's bracelet with a painful tug. Was that Jack over there? She glimpsed the back of a man who might have been him, leaping a table with two others in pursuit.

Her heart was thudding as people trampled along in their quest for the dance hall doors. She would be squashed, she was certain. She could hardly breathe as it was. Just as she felt herself sinking into the mass of bodies, her knees buckling beneath her, she was grabbed by the arm and hoisted out to the side. She struggled to right herself and pushed her hair from her face with a shaking hand. To her shock, she saw it was Agnes who had saved her.

'Thank you,' she gasped. 'I fell, I was going under.'

'You shouldn't be here,' Agnes snapped. 'This isn't for the likes of you. You should curse the guy who brought you. He doesn't care much for your safety.'

'He didn't know it would go like this,' Avril protested, defending Jack even as she wondered. Had he known it was such a rough place? Had he knowingly taken a risk, bringing her and Peggy here?

Agnes shook her head wearily. 'I'll get you out. There's a back door the band use. We can get through there.'

'How do you know that?' Avril shouted after her. Agnes hadn't waited to make sure she was following. Avril ran to catch her up, dodging two men circling each other.

'My boyfriend plays in the band,' Agnes said shortly. 'Now hurry up. I don't know why I'm even helping you.'

They ran together, against the stream of movement, down a side corridor and into a room at the back of the stage. It was silent and empty. Avril's ears were buzzing and she was dizzy. Agnes grabbed her shoulder and they went on to a plain, red painted door.

'Go out there, you'll be fine,' Agnes said, giving her a shove.

Avril stumbled out onto the street. She looked back at the young woman. 'What about you? You should come with me. It's dangerous in there.'

'Naw, my boyfriend's still in there. The fights'll be over soon enough and the band will step up again and start the music. Go home and don't come back here.'

'Thank you,' Avril called.

Agnes gave a brusque nod and then she was gone.

Avril looked around her, disorientated. She was nowhere near where they had originally queued. Where was Peggy? She prayed her friend was okay.

And what about Jack?

'Avril! Thank goodness I've found you.' A familiar deep voice broke into her dazed thoughts.

'Gordon! I can't believe it's you. How did you find me?' She wanted to cry with relief. She ran straight into his arms, surprising them both, and Gordon hugged her tightly as if he would never let her go.

She pulled away reluctantly. 'Have you seen Peggy? We have to find her. She might be injured or scared.'

'I've got her,' Gordon told her. 'She's waiting for us at the tram stop. She's hurt her ankle but she's okay apart from that. What on earth possessed you to come dancing here?'

'I didn't know it would be like this,' Avril wailed. 'Jack took us. Oh dear, where can he be?'

'Is he the fellow who came to visit Davey?' Gordon asked a little harshly.

'Yes — can you help me to find him?'

Gordon swore softly under his breath

and Avril pretended not to hear him. 'If I catch up with the scoundrel, I'll add a few more injuries to whatever he's got. What was he thinking, taking you two girls to a dump like this? It's a dangerous part of town. This is gang territory and as you've no doubt noticed, a gang fight has broken out around you. Now come along before it spills out onto the street.'

He put his arm protectively round her and guided her to the other side of the block, where a tearful Peggy was leaning against the tram stop shelter.

'Avril! You're okay! I lost sight of you in all the mess. Someone tripped over me and I've twisted my ankle. I was practically crawling out of the door when Gordon arrived and lifted me up.' Peggy's gaze at Gordon was even more loving than before. He was her hero who had rescued her.

Avril was absurdly glad when Gordon didn't take advantage of Peggy's cow's eyes.

'We need to get you home and put a

cold compress on your ankle,' he said firmly.

'What were *you* doing here?' Avril said suddenly.

Gordon blushed. The tram arrived and he helped them on. It wasn't until they'd paid their tickets and were trundling along in the direction of home that he was able to answer.

'Peggy happened to mention you were going dancing here tonight. I must admit that the name of the place didn't click with me right away. I'm not from Glasgow, but then I remembered one of the teachers in school talking about it. It's a dreadful place with a dark reputation. Once I realised that's where you'd gone I decided I'd better follow and persuade you to come home. I couldn't bear the thought of telling your parents if anything bad happened to either of you.'

He kindly included Peggy in this statement but Avril knew he meant her parents. He'd become very close to her dad through the stories about his own

171

father, which continued apace. He was polite and helpful to her mother too, and she responded by giving Gordon little extra titbits at dinner, earning him the wrath of Mr Phillips and doleful looks from Mrs Petrocelli.

The tram swayed on its lines and Avril swayed with it into Gordon. She giggled. There was nothing amusing, but she was glad they were safe. It was a release of tension.

He drew back. 'You've been drinking.'

'No, we haven't,' she protested. Come to mention it, though, she did feel a bit sick.

Peggy looked surprised. 'Jack must've added it to the juices. It did taste a bit off.'

'The devil,' Gordon growled.

Perhaps it was just as well that Jack had vanished, Avril thought sleepily. Gordon looked quite capable of killing him.

★   ★   ★

Peggy's house was dim and silent when they took her home. Avril managed to find a clean piece of cloth in the kitchen and soaked it in cold water to wrap round Peggy's ankle.

'Ouch!' Peggy yelped. 'That's arctic. Is that necessary?'

'If you want to stop the swelling getting worse, then yes. It's very purple already.'

Peggy lowered her voice so Gordon wouldn't hear from his stance in the hallway, waiting for Avril.

'Do you think Jack's okay? Did you see the knives?'

Avril shook her head, frightened for Jack. 'We could ask your brother Johnny tomorrow if he's seen him.'

'He kissed you, didn't he?' Peggy asked in a whisper.

Avril packed the compress tightly and concentrated on rolling a tea towel over it to secure it. Peggy yawned and lay back on the sofa. 'I'm going to sleep here tonight. Mum'll never notice, she doesn't get up 'til late.'

Avril mopped up spilt water drops. It was time to go to her own bed. She was bone weary.

'And Avril,' Peggy murmured. 'He likes you. Don't let him go. He's a keeper.'

She snored, lost in an instant to sleep. Avril wasn't so sure that Jack was a keeper. He was attractive and illicit, which was appealing, but he'd been quick to scarper tonight and leave them to fend for themselves. If he turned up, he'd have some explaining to do.

As she left the room, she realised Peggy's line of sight had been straight to Gordon's tall back, patiently waiting for her in the hallway. Had she been talking about him after all?

9

'Did you know that a new dish has been created especially for the new Queen? Coronation Chicken it's called, apparently. Now taste this. I've no idea what their recipe is, but I'm inventing my own version.'

Gordon could hear the triumph in Linda Garnett's voice and the ceramic clash of bowls and utensils from the kitchen.

'Mmm, that's delicious, Mum. Shall I add just a touch more pepper, though?'

How was it possible that just the sound of Avril's voice could lift his spirits and put a lightness to his tread? He was thankful yet again that he'd followed his instincts and gone to the dance hall the previous night. If something had happened to Avril — ! He tensed. It didn't bear thinking about. She'd become precious to him over the few weeks he'd lived in the boarding house. His feelings for her would never change, except to get deeper. He hugged them to him.

'Gordon, there you are,' Linda called, catching sight of him passing by the kitchen. 'We need your advice.'

He was taken into the kitchen and presented with a bowl of chicken smothered in a creamy, yellow sauce. Avril gave him a spoon with a dramatic flourish. 'Please try Mum's new dish. If it works, it's going to be the centrepiece on the trestle tables at the street party.'

There were blue shadows under her eyes today and her face was pale but cheerful. Gordon guessed she'd had a rotten night's sleep due to the effects of the alcohol. It made him livid that Jack had mixed the drinks. If he ever caught up with him . . .

He lifted a cautious spoonful of the chicken to his mouth, watched eagerly by two pairs of eyes. It was good, nicely savoury and faintly spicy.

'He likes it, I can tell,' Linda said proudly. 'So, that's the main dish organised. I've made a list, see, of which neighbour's bringing which dish of food to the party.'

She and Avril pored over her notes.

Gordon was going to make his escape when Linda's head shot up. 'I almost forgot. There were two letters for you yesterday, Gordon. They'd fallen down under the mat so I didn't see them when I collected the mail. Two in one day. Now that's got to be a record, even for you.'

She meant two from the same correspondent, of course. Lucille's letters were coming thick and fast, interspersed with tearful phone calls. She'd made him promise to telephone her. He had to walk up the road to do so and it was a regular outing. He was beginning to hate the pillar-box red with its associations of fear and guilt and sadness.

Avril was looking at him curiously. She lowered her gaze when he glanced back at her. She was too polite to ask about the letters and for that, he was immensely glad. He couldn't explain; he didn't have the right words to tell about Lucille.

'Excuse me,' he murmured.

The letters were propped up on the hallway table as usual. He slid them into his pocket for later. He couldn't read them now. He deserved a little respite, surely. Even him.

'Gordon?' Avril was standing behind him. He hadn't heard her step in her soft slippers. She wiped her hands unnecessarily on the front of her clean apron. He was conscious of her slightness and a wave of tenderness washed over him. The top of her head reached only to his shoulder. But when she turned her face up to talk to him, the beauty of her dark chocolate eyes made him want to kiss each eyelid and then her soft mouth. She reached into the long pocket of the embroidered apron and pulled out a thin notebook.

'I've finished the article. At least, I

think I have. Will you look at it for me? Could you check my spellings? Will you tell me if you think it's any good?' The words rushed from her all at once and a pretty pink flush tinged her cheeks.

'I'd be delighted,' he told her, taking the notebook carefully and sliding it in with Lucille's letters. Words, strong and powerful and positive mingling with those that were negative and aching and draining, between the paper sheets. Now he was being whimsical. He patted his jacket to indicate he had her notebook safe and heard the crackle and rasp of the words lined up for him to read.

Avril leaned towards him on tiptoe and briefly kissed his cheek. 'Thanks.'

There was a delicate scent of violets as he felt the feathery touch of a curl of her hair and the sweet warmth of her breath. Heat rose in him, and a fierce desire for her. He had to move away before his body betrayed him. But Avril was quicker. The kitchen door closed and he was left stunned, alone, in the hall.

It meant nothing, he argued. It was a token of friendship from her — that was all. And if he needed a reminder of why there was no hope for him, then Lucille's letters burning in his pocket fulfilled just that purpose.

* * *

He was returning from his daily visit to the river when he heard raised voices coming from the garden. Avril was there, talking with a man. He recognised Jack's tones from his visit to Davey. Knowing it was wrong, he stood to the side of the house and listened. He couldn't be seen unless they left the garden for the street. His fists clenched at Jack's appeasing comments.

'You've every right to be angry with me. I wouldn't blame you if you threw me out bodily and told me never to darken your door again. I feel terrible.'

'Don't be silly, Jack. I'm hardly going to throw you out. But I did wonder what happened to you. I was very worried — and Peggy was, too.'

'There was a bit of bother with a coupla groups. I got tangled up in it by mistake. Before I knew it, there I was on the floor with a knock to my head. See, feel the bump.'

Feel the bump. Gordon's knuckles ached. What an excuse! The fellow was a louse, pure and simple.

Avril's voice softened. 'Poor you. That looks nasty. Anyway, it all ended well, apart from Peggy getting a twisted ankle. Luckily my friend Gordon was in the neighbourhood and took us home.'

There was an ominous silence. Gordon imagined this piece of information sinking in to Jack's brain. He wouldn't like it. Gordon found himself grinning. It was absurd, eavesdropping like a lovelorn schoolboy and wanting to hear good about himself from Avril's perfect lips.

'Who's Gordon? It's not the lodger, is it? The worn-looking one with the bad limp?'

Gordon ground his teeth. They did say eavesdroppers never heard good about themselves. It served him right. He was being foolish. He'd just wanted a signal — some sort of sign that would tell him how Avril felt about Jack.

'Gordon is our new lodger, yes.' There was a crunch of gravel as if they'd moved closer. 'Jack, can we start afresh? Don't ask me to forgive you for last night because there's nothing to forgive. I can see now you were badly hurt. I'm only glad you managed to get out of there and avoid the knives.'

'How about I make it up to you?' Jack had perked up. 'Fancy going to the pictures?'

Avril hesitated. There was a burst of birdsong before her reply. Gordon was reminded of the blackbird's nest and Avril's delight in it.

'That sounds nice. Could Peggy come, too? She's a bit down in the dumps because of her leg.'

'Lovely, just lovely. That's settled, then.' Some of the cockiness had been knocked out of Jack at the mention of including Peggy. The crunch of gravel got louder.

Gordon nipped round to the front of the house as if he'd just arrived. He was no clearer on Avril's feelings for Jack.

'Hello,' he greeted them politely.

Avril smiled happily at him. Jack scowled then hid it under a thin-lipped twist of a smile. The air bristled subtly between the two men.

'Jack was just leaving.'

Jack touched a finger to forehead in a salute and went off whistling with bravado.

'Is he someone special?' Gordon heard himself asking.

'He's a . . . friend,' Avril said hesitantly. She plucked a petal from her cardigan, where it had fallen off the laden cherry tree in the garden. 'A good friend.'

There seemed to Gordon to be a strong emphasis on 'good'. *What is it to me anyway?* he thought savagely. He couldn't have Avril. It didn't matter that he'd fallen in love with her. She should find happiness elsewhere. He muttered his excuses and left her there, angry with himself.

★   ★   ★

Lucille had a gift for opening up his memories. *Do you remember* . . . she wrote and he was at once transported back to those days when he and Ronnie were young and brimful with life. There were many memories to choose from and Lucille played them like a pack of cards, fanned and ready to pick.

They'd had adventures and scrapes as boys growing up together, best friends forever. Lucille, Ronnie's little sister, had tagged along, tolerated and looked out for but never needed. In her mind only, the synergy had shifted once they reached their teens and early adulthood.

She'd visited him at home one day in the village. Gordon was surprised. He was by then in his twenties, studying hard to take his teaching exams in the hope of becoming the master of the local primary school.

'Ronnie's not here,' he said, thinking she was looking for her brother. For he was the connection between them.

'It's not Ronnie I'm looking for,' Lucille said boldly, stepping forward so that he had to take an equal step back or share the same physical space. Her long, red hair shone in the weak northern light and her pale blue eyes flashed. He was suddenly acutely aware of her womanhood. She was no longer the little girl running after them and shouting for them to wait. Now she was full-busted and wide-hipped, curved and plump and dewy with a dangerous promise. She ran the tip of her tongue over her top lip. Like a cat's fur, he was abruptly tuned to danger.

'I'm working. I don't have time to talk,' he said harshly.

Lucille ignored this remark. 'You know why I've come. We've known each other too long to tiptoe round with words. I've loved you forever, Gordon Silver, and you love me too. I'm finished with waiting!' She rubbed up against him.

He was aghast. It was all wrong. He pushed her too forcefully and she staggered, her mouth falling open in astonishment.

Wretchedly he stared at her. 'I do love you, Lucille — but as a sister. I've never promised you anything else. I don't feel that way about you — how could I? We grew up together as family.'

She'd gone pale, her Celtic freckles brown-flecked on the planes of her cheeks. A sheen of bright tears covered her eyes. Without a word, she turned and fled. He felt absolutely dreadful.

After a few minutes, he followed her, calling her name. When he caught up with her, apologising over and over, she stopped him. He thought she was going to agree with him, that she'd made a terrible mistake but she understood how he felt. But she stared him down. She was a tall woman, on a

186

par with his own height.

'You're wrong, Gordon. You do love me and one day you'll come to realise it. I can wait, after all.'

They had never spoken of it again, but it was there like an undercurrent when all three of them got together. After the tragedy of Ronnie's death, Lucille had gone to pieces and Gordon had been there to look after her. He had owed it to Ronnie to care for Lucille.

Eventually, though, it became too much. Gordon knew he had to leave the Highlands or risk sinking into a dark morass from which he would never recover, because Lucille's grief was overpowering. As the months went by, he noticed a change in her. She was too close, touching him whenever she could. He feared she was becoming too attached to him — unhealthily so. He could never give her what she wanted.

He'd hoped that in his absence she would grow closer to her parents, who so clearly needed her now Ronnie was gone. So he'd packed his bags and left for Glasgow. Now she kept him on a long string with her letters and calls.

He scanned to the end of the second letter quickly as the gong for dinner rang. He fumbled, catching the paper as it peeled away, fluttering down in a wafer-thin layer.

Lucille's last sentences.

I've had enough of this place and of my parents nagging me to get on with life. Don't they understand I don't want to move on without Ronnie? I need a break, and so I've decided I'm coming to visit you. I've booked a hotel in Glasgow so you needn't worry about where I shall stay. I've missed you — but soon we'll be together again.

Lucille was coming to Glasgow and there was nothing he could do about it.

10

Avril was glad it was Monday and that Gordon had gone to work. The front door had been slammed with some force that morning, making Linda frown. Gordon had been in an odd mood since meeting Jack, if she thought about it. Or perhaps it was connected to the letters he kept getting.

Whatever the reason, the strangest part of it was that he appeared to be angry with himself. He was perfectly pleasant to everyone, if a little withdrawn. She shook her head; no, she couldn't fathom it. She only hoped that whatever it was had worn off by the time he came home from school, because she was dying to ask him what he thought of her written article.

On impulse, she'd reached up and given him a friendly kiss on the cheek as a kind of thank you for taking an interest in her project. She hadn't expected the tingling sensation on her lips at the feel of his stubbled, male jaw, nor the zap of electricity which went right through her.

He'd felt it too, she was sure of it. He'd jumped away from her like a scalded cat. She'd run away to the kitchen, confused and unsure what it meant. She valued his friendship so much and only hoped she hadn't lost it by that innocent action. She finished brushing her hair, made a face at herself in the mirror and scampered lightly down the stairs.

There were happy, childish voices coming from the dining room. Avril peeked in and was astonished. Around the table were Gloria, Shirley — and Helen. In front of them was a tiered cake stand with thin buttered sand-wiches and dainty iced buns.

'Avril, come in and have a cake,' Gloria called out, catching sight of her.

'We're having a very early high tea,' Shirley giggled, ramming a luridly

190

pink-topped bun into her mouth.

Helen giggled too, but Avril noticed she was eating her bun in tiny pieces, savouring each morsel.

'That's nice,' she answered cautiously. 'Did Mum make these for you?'

'Yes, and there's a second batch coming soon so you should stay,' Gloria advised seriously.

'I'll go and help Mum with it,' Avril said.

Linda was in the kitchen, icing the last of the buns. She looked up and her careworn face relaxed in a smile.

'That's the last of the sugar ration for this week. Still, it's gone to a good cause. Did you see that little girl's face when she saw the buns? Worth every ounce of my sugar!'

Avril simply stared at her mother. Every time she was certain she had her pinned, Linda amazed her.

'You don't mind her keeping company with Gloria and Shirley, then?' she asked.

Linda raised her eyebrows, 'I can't

say I was too happy to start with. I was worried they might catch something in their hair. It wasn't nice of me, but I put their welfare first. That's what being a mother's about.' She turned the newly iced buns onto a tray, complete with paper doilies underneath. 'But when Gloria told me about Helen's family and the awful cramped space they have to live in, I looked at her in a different way. I felt sorry for her. My goodness, if a little cake cheers her up so much, it's the least I can do. The Queen doesn't distinguish between all her subjects, does she? If that attitude's good enough for her, it's good enough for me.'

With this majestic speech, she swept past Avril on a swell of compassion and fragrant sugar. Linda Garnett was a great fan of the new, young Queen. She could do no wrong. In fact, Avril realised, the Queen's Coronation was going to be one of the highlights of her mother's life.

She was determined, from that

moment, to help make it a memorable occasion for all of them. She would start by visiting Dad and making sure that he was going to get involved and support Mum. She swiped a couple of buns that had been left cooling on a wire rack, and headed for the allotment.

* * *

She hadn't been to the plot for a few days and the crops were shooting up. Very little bare earth was visible amongst the bushy leaves and green netting. She looked for her father, thinking he would be weeding or hoeing the rows.

A loud clatter came from the shed and she hurried forward in case he'd fallen, but before she could go in, the door to the shed swung open and her father came out backwards, dragging what looked like large pieces of wood.

'Ah, Avril! Give me a hand, would you? There should be two or three more of these at the back. Bert's got some, too. He's coming over soon to help repair them.'

Avril saw then that the wood was actually old trestle tables. The paint was flaking off them and some hinges were hanging off. But they were salvageable, if creaky with age.

'Where did you get these, Dad?'

'You don't remember? What age would you have been? Thirteen? The end of the war, VE Day. We had the greatest street party ever. Aline Street knows how to celebrate — and it won't be any different this time round.'

'I do remember,' Avril exclaimed. 'It was such fun. Everyone was so happy. I ate three paste sandwiches and was sick on my shoes.'

'It didn't stop you eating more and having a right old time of it, if I recall.' Her father chuckled, rubbing his hands together. 'Right — it's down to some serious renovation work now.'

Avril went into the shed, fumbling about in the sudden dimness after the bright daylight. It smelt of familiar things; damp earth, clay pots, the dustiness of rooting powder and of course ingrained pipe smoke. Yet when she put her fingers on the pipe, lying idle on the shelf, it was cold. Dad was so engrossed in his task, he hadn't lit it up today.

She found two more old tables, managed to carefully free them from the tangled paraphernalia and bring them out to the little patioed area.

'Mum's very keen on the Coronation celebrations,' she said, tentatively. How should she broach the subject of Dad leaving his allotment for a whole day?

David's back was to her, bent over inspecting a broken strut. There was a hole in his old gardening jersey. It was frayed and getting larger each time she visited. For some reason it made her want to hug him, to cry out, *Don't get old, Dad. Always be here, just like this, where I'm safe with you.* Because the allotment was just that; a safe place. It was her father's haven, certainly, but Avril instinctively came here too when she needed a place. But without Dad, it was nothing.

'Yes, she's very keen,' he agreed, straightening up from his task, coughing at the exertion and patting his top pocket for his missing pipe.

'We must all make it a great success,' Avril went on. 'For Mum's sake.'

David sat down. Avril brought him his pipe but he didn't light it immediately. Instead he laid it down slowly on his lap, one gnarled finger keeping it steady and in place. The whorled, seasoned wood matched the browned whorls of his knuckles where the soil had ingrained itself.

'It will be a success *because of* Mum,' he said. 'She's a determined lady, you know. Always has been. Very strong-minded on all sorts of topics — even as a girl, when I met her.' He chuckled softly. 'It didn't make for an easy courtship, but it was never dull. You remind me of her.'

'Me — like Mum?' Avril had never thought of it. She would have said they were complete opposites. Mum was a house-maker, a mother, while she was . . . she didn't know what, yet.

'Your Mum's made a success of her life. She's channelled all her energies into bringing up four lovely children we can be proud of. She provides us with a clean home and good food and she works too, to compensate for my frailties. I don't know what I'd do without her.'

And there it was. A simple statement of true love. It wasn't all glitter and drama like the movies, but it was solid and real and everlasting. It was worth having. Avril experienced a novel flash of envy for her parents. What would it be like to never be alone, to never be lonely? To have a soul mate?

'What I'm trying to say, love, is that you'll make a success of your life, too. It hasn't escaped me that you've been troubled lately and restless. But you're calmer today. Something's changed, has it?'

He was right. Her restlessness and

197

boredom had vanished. She could have said it was her writing that had done it, but there was more to it. She wasn't seeking excitement any more because it had come to her. She was enjoying her meetings with Jack — that was it — and in addition she had a good friend in Gordon. She could talk to him so easily. Jack was more interested in having a good time. She liked that too, of course, but on its own its novelty began to pall.

'So Dad, you will be at the street party, won't you?' she asked quickly, setting her musings aside.

He stopped his hammering and looked at her in astonishment.

'I wouldn't miss it! Between you and me, I'd rather sit here and watch my veg grow, but I'd never let your mother down. No, no, I'll be there, love. Now I must get on with doing this, or there won't be any tables — and without tables it's unlikely to be much of a party because there'll be nowhere to put the food.'

He kissed the top of her head. Avril

knew when she was being dismissed. She gave him one of the iced buns, and set the other down for Bert who was making his way laboriously towards them. He had trestles too, and Avril remembered Bert's fine singing on VE day when he'd entertained them all with heartfelt lyrics from Vera Lynn's popular songs.

★　★　★

Peggy was stretched out languidly on the sofa when Avril popped by to visit.

'How's the ankle?'

'It's rubbish! I can't put any weight on it and I'm bored of lying here,' her friend answered sulkily.

'Well, these should cheer you up. Shirley sent them.' Avril threw a bag of sticky sweets at her friend.

Peggy's cheek bulged as she chewed on a toffee and offered the bag to Avril. 'At least I had a couple of visitors yesterday. Everyone's too busy today to care about me.'

199

'Hey, I'm visiting you right now,' Avril protested.

'Apart from you.' Peggy hoisted herself up so she was sitting upright, and helped herself to another sweet. 'Don't you want to know who came visiting?'

'The Queen? She's making a variety of tours round the country in the run up to the Coronation. I expect she decided to fit you in specially.'

Peggy threw the bag at Avril's head and there was a dull clunk as it connected. 'Ha! Got you! No, not the Queen, you idiot. It was Jack.'

'Jack?' He must have gone straight round to Peggy's house after leaving her yesterday.

'Yes. He said he'd come to apologise for Saturday evening but he spent most of the time talking about you. Oh, and asking questions about Gordon. Who he was, what he was to you, what did you think about him. Honestly, he went on and on. It was very boring. In fact I almost wished he hadn't even bothered coming to visit me. Especially when he said you and him were going out to the cinema together this week. He made it quite plain it was a proper date. I felt like a gooseberry just hearing about it.'

Jack Lafferty was a sly one. A cold shiver went up Avril's spine, chased away in a whisper. A ghost was passing, her granny would have claimed. All of a sudden, she didn't want to be alone with Jack in a cinema on a 'proper date'.

'It isn't a proper date at all,' she said firmly to Peggy. 'We aren't going steady.'

'That's not the way Jack tells it.'

'I told him quite clearly that I wanted to invite you out to the cinema too, to cheer you up,' Avril said heatedly. 'I want you to come along. In fact, you have to.'

'So what is the deal between you and Jack?' Peggy asked.

Avril sighed. 'I don't know yet. Why does it have to rush along so fast? Can't we enjoy a few outings and get to know each other better that way?'

'Jack's certainly keen to get to know you,' Peggy muttered darkly. 'But I'm guessing that his motives are running differently from yours.'

'Oh, bother him,' Avril said rudely. 'Let's forget him. Who else visited?'

Peggy snuggled down under her light blanket. 'Your Davey came to see me. He'd written a song for me.' She snorted with laughter. 'It was very funny — all about how beautiful I was even with my tragically broken leg.'

Poor Davey. He'd probably stayed up all night working on the melody and the lyrics, and putting his whole heart into his song for Peggy.

'Was it . . . meant to be humorous?' Avril asked delicately.

Peggy looked surprised. 'I think so. It got me laughing. I told him it was wonderful, that he'd cheered me up no end.'

She swallowed a large piece of toffee and coughed until tears came to her eyes. Avril thumped her on the back.

There was a brief silence. Then Peggy spoke, sounding slightly guilty. 'Gosh, do you think it was serious? It's just . . . honestly, Avril, the words were unbelievable. You should ask him to play it to you, you won't recognise the descriptions of me. My swan-like neck and my eyes like great blue saucers.' Peggy hiccupped and was off again, laughing uncontrollably.

It was cruel, Avril reflected, when you loved someone but it wasn't reciprocated. Peggy was never going to see Davey as anything other than her next-door neighbour and Avril's big brother. She only hoped that, in time, Davey would outgrow his calf love for Peggy.

* * *

She left her friend much cheered up, and with the firm promise of the cinema trip. It was late afternoon, and there was time before dinner to follow her favourite route down by the trickling, culverted stream to the river walkway.

She stopped as she turned the curve which would give the fine view of the great river all spread out before her. There was someone else on the path today. A tall figure who turned at her footsteps. It was Gordon.

She went quickly towards him, glad to see him and hopeful that his strange mood had dispersed.

'I didn't think to see you here. I know you hate the water,' Avril exclaimed.

'I made a pact with myself,' Gordon explained. 'I'll come here every day until I no longer feel that revulsion and fear.'

'That's marvellous. Is it working? Do you feel better?'

'Not better, not yet,' he admitted, 'But I'm here. That's the start of it. I talk to the river. It's crazy, I know, but I feel one day it'll answer back and I'll be free of it.'

It didn't sound crazy at all to Avril. She knew what he was trying to say.

He changed the subject clumsily. 'I read your article. It's very good. You can send it off.'

'Just like that?' she said warily.

'Just like that.' He repeated her words, making them into a command, school teacher-like.

'I'm scared,' Avril confessed.

'Of what? Your mother finding out? Or of failure?'

She wasn't scared any more of her mother finding out. With her recently gained insight into her character, she suspected Linda might even be proud of her for trying. But, being Mum, Avril was never sure which way she'd jump. It was best to be cautious. Fear of failure, however, was another thing altogether.

'Yes — what if it turns out to be no good after all, and my dream of writing is over before it's begun?' she whispered.

'You have to try. It's all any of us can do,' Gordon declared, indicating the river.

She got it. He was right. He was challenging himself each day to overcome his fear of water. He had no way of knowing when, or even if, it would work, but he did it anyway. And so could she.

He gave her the paper and she took it steadily.

Before them on the river a steamer went by, puffs of smoke rising like clouds into the sky.

'Would you like to walk with me?' Avril asked. 'I'm going along the path for a little while until it's time to turn back for dinner. There are some flowers coming out along under the bridge. I don't know what they're called but they've gorgeous yellow blossoms.'

Gordon looked torn.

'Sorry.' Avril touched his arm. 'That was thoughtless of me. You've probably had enough of the water for one day.'

When he didn't answer, she asked gently, 'Is it Ronnie? Are you thinking about him?'

Gordon made a strangled sound. He

rubbed his face wearily. 'I think about him all the time when I'm at the river. But it's all that I deserve. It's a penance.'

'I don't understand. What do you mean, it's a penance? Why do you deserve to suffer so much?'

'Because it's all my fault,' Gordon blurted out. His eyes were red-rimmed as he stared wildly at her. 'The accident was entirely my fault.'

Avril shook her head. 'How could it be your fault? It was just that, an accident. You told me yourself that the car slid down an embankment into a river. It was a terrible freak occurrence. Why do you torture yourself so?'

She tried to hold him, desperate to give him comfort, but he turned from her, gazing blindly at the far shore, a dark streak across the slow river water.

'I killed him. I murdered Ronnie. As much as if I'd taken up a gun or a knife to him.'

'No, that's not true!' Avril cried.

'Yes, it is.' The words were torn from

him. 'I was young and stupid and I was driving too fast, showing off. We were going at such a speed we were never going to make the corner. The car slewed round and I let go of the wheel. It was over in seconds. Ronnie never stood a chance.'

Gordon was white and shaking. Avril acted on instinct. She hurled herself at him fiercely and held him tight, ignoring his attempts to get free, until he calmed in her arms. She could feel his heart pounding in his chest as she laid her head on it, her arms wrapped around him.

'You were young and reckless and over-confident like all young men but you're not a murderer,' she said savagely. 'It was a terrible, awful, tragic accident but that's what it was. You're not to blame. You suffered, too. And it's only a matter of luck, or the turn of a dice, that you survived and Ronnie didn't. It could just as easily have been the other way round. Or what if he'd driven badly that day? Would you have blamed him? I know you wouldn't.'

She looked up at him, willing her words to affect him and caught his gaze. Without thinking, she kissed his lips, softly, so softly. A liquid heat suffused her body and she pulled his head down to hers more closely.

Gordon groaned and his mouth upon hers was mobile and tender until his kiss became urgent and seeking. She felt the length of his body against hers and wanted more, so much more. They took from each other hungrily, oblivious to the lapping water and the breeze and the cries of the river birds.

Gordon drew a ragged breath and lifted his head from hers. 'Avril,' he whispered and she thought her name had never sounded so sweet upon anyone's lips. She said nothing but gently cupped her hands around the strong column of his neck and pulled him in for a kiss at once insistent and searching but also tender and loving and passionate.

11

The kiss had shaken them both. Avril hadn't expected it, and neither had Gordon. It had come like a bolt from the blue, searing them with its power. Avril could only think of Gordon. She stood in front of her mirror, getting ready to go to the cinema with Jack and Peggy, trying on one smile after another in a bid to hide her unhappiness.

She replayed the scene again, running it in her mind like a series of frames or in slow motion. They had kissed, and when it was done, Avril was changed forever. Gordon wasn't just a friend — he was so much more.

She was in love with him. Her heart should be singing with joy. But he had looked at her with torment and told her that it couldn't be, that it was a mistake, that they could only be friends. He had nothing to offer her. When she'd argued, he'd mutely shaken his head and left her there on the river path. Since then, he had avoided her.

So she would put on a brave face and go out to the cinema when all she wanted to do was lie on her bed and cry. She wouldn't give up on him, but she needed space before she approached him. When she had gathered the courage to do so, she wanted answers from him as to why it wouldn't work.

It was all somehow linked to the guilt he had surrounding Ronnie's death, but that wasn't good enough for Avril. She needed to shake the guilt free from him so that he could move on. With her. With stronger resolve, she applied a thin curve of pale lipstick and went downstairs to find Peggy.

'What's up with you?' Peggy asked. She was sitting on a chair in the hall, favouring her sore ankle. The swelling had gone down and she could squeeze her foot into a normal shoe, but it was still tender.

'Is it that obvious?' Avril said weakly. She sat down next to Peggy to compose herself.

'Something's happened. Let me guess!' Peggy's eyes lit up. There was nothing she liked more than a slice of intrigue layered with gossip. 'It's Gordon, isn't it? You two have hit it off. But wait, that's not it — or else why do you look so miserable?'

'It is Gordon — but it's complicated.' Avril kept her voice low, even though she knew for a fact that Gordon had gone out earlier that evening.

'Oooh, do tell.' Peggy leaned in, crossing her legs and forgetful of her ankle. She winced, but rested her elbow on knee and chin in palm, indicating her readiness to listen.

'I think I'm in love with him,' Avril lamented.

'And you told him that and he ran a mile,' Peggy surmised.

'How did you know?'

Peggy patted her knee kindly. 'You don't know much about men, do you,

Avril? Here's a tip — always keep them guessing. You've frightened Gordon off. Men like to do the running. Your job is to flirt and be nice until he's desperate to know what you're thinking about him. Eventually it gets too much and he asks you out — or goes straight to it and asks you to marry him. Look what happened when I asked Gordon out dancing. Although as it turns out, he wasn't interested in me anyway.'

'I don't want to play those games,' Avril cried. 'I love Gordon. It's as simple as that.'

She didn't want to explain to Peggy about Gordon's accident and his guilt over Ronnie. That wasn't her story to tell. Some of what Peggy said made a kind of sense, but Avril knew there was more to it. Gordon wasn't the kind to play games. He was straightforward.

'Where does that leave Jack?' Peggy asked.

Avril hadn't considered Jack at all. She'd not thought of him since kissing Gordon. Her attraction to him seemed shallow now, only skin-deep. She hadn't discovered any of his depths during their conversations. She admitted to herself that his magnetism was all surface looks, and that element of danger she sensed around him. It was what she had needed then — but not now.

'I like Jack,' she answered. 'He's good company and entertaining. But I don't love him.'

'You could do worse, though,' Peggy commented. 'I mean, if Gordon isn't interested in you or if you've scared him off. Jack's fun — he's never dull. He's good-looking and well-heeled and he likes you a lot. Jack would do.'

'Jack would do what exactly?' Jack enquired, arriving at the doorway and leaning in, reluctant to come right in to the house in case Davey cornered him.

'Oh, Jack would be good company for two girls dying to see the new film out at the cinema,' Peggy improvised gaily, winking broadly at Avril.

She had to make an effort to smile

and laugh in the right places as they chatted and strolled along to the cinema. Peggy was slow-moving and Avril wished she could pick her friend up and run to the pictures so that she could hide in the darkness, and then be home again to mull over her situation alone.

Instead it took ages to get there, and they had to queue round the block before they got in to buy their tickets and a box of chocolate mint creams to share. Jack sat between them when they reached the rubbed velvet seats, and she hoped he'd keep his hands to himself.

Poor Jack — it wasn't his fault she'd had a change of heart. She promised herself she'd find a way to let him know she was no longer interested. But it had to be done in a kindly and sensitive manner so as not to hurt him. Avril sighed in the warm wrap of the dark cinema hall. Why was life so complicated?

Jack pretended to stretch and tentatively laid his arm along the top of

Avril's seat. It was wonderfully dark apart from the flickering light from the huge screen, and he hoped the passionate embrace of the two main characters would inspire Avril in his direction. He let his hand drop casually where his fingertips could make contact with her shoulder and waited for a response. Even this slight touch set his nerve-endings tingling. He really had it bad for this particular girl.

Jack couldn't understand it. He had girls falling over him at the dance halls and they evoked none of the sensations he was feeling now. What was it about Avril Garnett? Was it her soft, unblemished skin, her thick, brown hair or her soulful dark eyes?

Avril tensed at his closeness and reluctantly Jack took his arm off her chair. Perhaps it was her very inaccessibility that drew him to her. The ice-maiden, untouchable and unawakened.

'Great film, eh?' he whispered loudly into her ear.

Now if that was Belle or Ruby, they would giggle and curl in to him. But because it was Avril she merely nodded and smiled sweetly at him before her eyes flicked quickly back to the action on the film. Bored, Jack watched too. The villain, for some reason he'd missed, was kidnapping the heroine. She squealed but then fell head over heels for him. It was a rubbish film, but a spark of an idea seeded in his mind.

Jack was losing his touch. That much was clear to him. Avril was less interested every time he met her, while the opposite was true for him.

Then there was the problem of Shorty. He'd been lucky a bump on the head was all he got, that Saturday night at the dance hall. Shorty and Gibbs had taken advantage of the gang fight to chase him and rough him up. Gibbs had held him while Shorty gave his head a good thump on the hard floor.

'That's for making me wait for my money,' he snarled, while Gibbs grinned like a squat toad.

'I'm getting it as fast as I can. I wouldn't want you to be put out,' Jack smarmed, even from his uncomfortable position on the ground.

Shorty grunted.

'Let me up and I'll go right now and speed my contact up,' Jack wheedled.

Shorty jerked his head and Gibbs let go of him. Jack rolled his shoulders to ease the muscles and flexed his neck. Gibbs was a considerable weight. He straightened his jacket, making sure the velvet collar was pristine. These things mattered when you were on a charm offensive.

'You'd better have it next time I come calling,' Shorty said and there was no mistaking the cold menace in his voice.

Jack shivered. He couldn't charm his way out this predicament. The worst of it was, there was no money. It had run out — and with it Jack's hopes of escaping Shorty's retribution. Looking at the kidnapped heroine on screen, being released by the hero and falling in love with her captor, Jack realised there was only one way out.

He had to leave, and fast. He had to regain control of his life, which had frayed beyond repair. A fresh start was required. He drummed his fingers on his leg and thought about it. Where could he go where he could make money fast? Where did he have contacts? Where, too, could he disappear to where Shorty and his cronies could never find him?

He snapped his fingers, earning a frown from Peggy. That was it! He'd go back to London, see his old man, stay for free until he got sorted. There wouldn't be much of a welcome, but he'd survive. Dad might even have a caper or two he could join in.

He glanced over at Avril's perfect profile. How could he persuade her to go with him? What did all girls want?

To get married. Then that's what he would offer her.

He gulped. He wasn't the marrying kind, but if he couldn't have her otherwise, then he had to do it. It was the only way to get her to accompany him.

Gretna Green was on the route to London. A nasty little notion slipped into his head. He didn't actually have to marry her. One night alone with a man, however innocently, was sufficient to ruin a good girl's reputation. Avril would have to stay with him then. There could be no going back for her.

Any ambivalence he felt about his idea dissolved within seconds. Jack Lafferty put his own needs first. He'd learned early on that it was the only way to survive.

★   ★   ★

There was something antsy about Jack tonight, Avril thought with mild irritation. He'd spoiled the film for her with his whispering and drumming and the annoying crack of his fingers. She was glad when it was time to go home, and thankful for Peggy's presence as a buffer between them. She had to tell him, and soon, that she was no longer interested. She used Peggy's leg as an excuse and suggested they take a side of her each to help her home.

Jack was strangely upbeat despite her disinterest.

'I've decided to visit my old man down in London,' he remarked as they sauntered home. 'Nice to spend a bit of time with the family.'

Avril thought that was odd. Hadn't Jack told her he didn't get along with his father? 'A handful' — wasn't that the expression he'd used? He'd hinted that his dad was the reason his mother and sister had both fled the family.

Then, with relief, she realised this could be the solution. With Jack gone for a while, she could sort out her emotions and when he returned it wouldn't be too difficult to suggest they stay just friends, nothing more.

'That's lovely. When are you going?' Avril asked enthusiastically, then wondered whether her words had made it too obvious she wanted him gone.

'Soon,' he said vaguely.

'I've always fancied seeing London,' Peggy chipped in. 'Buckingham Palace and the Tower of London and everything. Lucky you, you'll get to see the Coronation procession for real. Is that why you're going?'

'Eh, yes. That's right, Peggy. You nailed it,' Jack said cheerfully. 'Two birds with one stone and all that. See the new Queen and me old Dad all at once.'

'I didn't know you were so interested in the Queen's Coronation,' Avril said, surprised. Jack hadn't shown much enthusiasm when she'd chatted about the forthcoming Aline Street party.

'There's lots of things you don't know about me,' Jack said mysteriously.

* * *

Avril left them at the door of the boarding house with thanks for the evening. Jack needed a word with

222

Johnny, so was going next door to Peggy's house. She put him out of her mind immediately, thankful to be home. The hallway was dim and quiet. It was late, and the family and lodgers had obviously retired to bed.

'Avril?' A voice spoke in the gloom.

'Gordon! You scared me.'

'Sorry. I couldn't sleep so I came down to get a glass of water. How are you?' Gordon was still dressed, but his shirt was open-necked and his fair hair sticking up, uncombed.

'I'm . . . fine.'

What else could she say? Would screaming out 'I love you' change anything?

Gordon's eyes were anguished. 'Avril, about the other day. I said things that were hurtful, and for that I apologise. But I need you to understand that I'm all churned up right now. I can't promise you anything.'

Avril felt a surge of love for him. 'You don't have to promise me anything. You can take your time to think things through. It was only a kiss, after all.'

It wasn't only a kiss to her. It had opened her eyes fully to the fact she was in love with him. But she couldn't expect the same response from him, could she?

'It was a wonderful kiss,' Gordon said quietly. 'You're a beautiful and desirable woman, Avril, and you deserve to be happy. I can't offer you that right now.'

No declaration of love from him. No promises. But Avril was buoyed anyway. He hadn't rejected her outright and she was confident he could work through his emotions. He was stronger than he knew.

'I'm not asking you to provide my happiness. But please let's be friends. I've missed you the last few days,' Avril said softly.

'We are friends,' Gordon assured her.

A creaking floorboard upstairs made them both look up beyond the banister. It would be inappropriate to be caught like this so late at night. They were both aware of it. With a lopsided smile to her, Gordon padded up the stairs and away.

She would not give up on him. Gordon's inner strength would prevail, and when it did, she was going to be there for him. She loved him. When he allowed himself happiness, she would be there to share it.

12

On Monday morning, Avril was in the same happy frame of mind. Her natural optimism had reasserted itself over the weekend. When the doorbell rang, she ran to answer it. She opened the door to find a tall, buxom woman standing there, her long, red hair streaming to her waist.

'I'm Lucille. I've come to visit my fiancé, Gordon Silver. Is he here?'

'There must be some mistake,' Avril blurted out.

'There's no mistake. Why should there be? Gordon didn't tell you he had a fiancée? Most good boarding houses don't allow single men female visitors, do they? I expect that's why he's kept quiet about me.'

The tall woman pushed past Avril into the hallway and looked around with interest. 'Where is he, then? I told

226

him I was coming down to see him. He should be here.'

'He's out working. He's a teacher, he can't just take days off at short notice,' Avril said, trying desperately to take in what Lucille's presence meant. Gordon had a fiancée! No wonder he was so tormented after kissing Avril. He was cheating on Lucille and his conscience — what there was of one — had been pricked.

'Who are you?' Lucille demanded.

'My mother runs the boarding house. I'm the help.'

'But you like him, too?' Lucille guessed, staring at Avril astutely as if sizing her up. 'You've been taken in by him, haven't you? Oh, he's a smooth one, all right. Did he tell you he was single? I can't believe you fell for it — a handsome man like that having no attachments. It's unlikely and it's certainly untrue. I'm the proof.'

Avril was stunned. Then her good sense returned. She trusted Gordon. She loved him. What kind of love was it, if she doubted him at the first hurdle? True, Lucille's appearance and claim to be Gordon's fiancée had thrown her, but there was bound to be an explanation. She had only to discover it.

Lucille had peeled off her gloves and draped them over her handbag. Now she unbuttoned her coat as if quite at home, and handed it to Avril.

'Hang this up for me, will you? Once you've done that, I'd like to see Gordon's room, please.'

The coat was dusty from her long journey and a light fragrance of lemon clung to it, Lucille's perfume. Avril was tempted to fling the coat on the floor and stamp on it, but with steeled grace she hung it from the brass coatstand hook and folded her arms.

'Perhaps you'd like to wait in the living room for Gordon. It will be quite some hours before he's home.'

'That won't be necessary, thank you. I'll have a look at his room and then I'll come back later this evening to see him. Once he knows I'm here, he'll be eager to catch up with me.'

Lucille's voice left nothing to the imagination. Avril imagined Gordon kissing her and winding her long red hair around his hand. She felt such a shaft of pain deep inside her chest that she struggled against it.

'I find it odd that Gordon hasn't mentioned you at all,' she said, with a hint of challenge.

Lucille shrugged. 'Gordon and I are both recovering from my brother's death last year. I forgive him if he hasn't spoken about me, I really do. He has a lot on his plate to deal with right now, as do I. We're grieving together and while it brings us ever closer and emotionally together, it's a painful journey.'

Her voice broke on the last sentence, and compassionate-hearted Avril felt awful for her.

'You're Ronnie's sister?'

Lucille blew her nose on a silk handkerchief and turned pale, wet eyes on Avril incredulously.

'Gordon's told you about Ronnie?'

'Yes . . . yes, he has,' Avril told her gently. 'I'm so sorry for your loss.'

'It's such a private hurt — I can't believe he told you about the accident.' Lucille looked at her with new wariness. 'Did he tell you he was driving when they crashed?'

Avril nodded.

Lucille said quickly, 'I've never blamed him for it, not once. It wouldn't bring Ronnie back.'

But there were other ways to accuse someone without words, Avril thought, noting the set of Lucille's rigid back and the tension of her jaw as she denied blaming Gordon.

Subconsciously, Lucille *did* blame Gordon. It was there to read in her body language. Gordon would pick up on it and relive his own guilt upon each encounter with Lucille. Was that why he'd chosen to have a relationship with this particular woman? Avril wondered.

She gave herself a mental shake. Lucille was too persuasive. She refused to believe the woman's claims until she'd spoken to Gordon herself.

But he told you he couldn't offer you anything, a little voice in her head reminded her. *He hasn't lied to you.*

His only crime was in kissing her. She had only herself to blame for falling so heavily for him after one perfect kiss. Had he tried to tell her about Lucille when he'd cried out that he'd made a mistake and that it could never work? Avril's head buzzed and she felt sick.

Lucille was talking again. 'Is Gordon's room upstairs? You needn't come. I'll find it. I've a sixth sense when it comes to my darling Gordon.'

There was no way Avril was letting Lucille loose upstairs.

'Very well, I'll show you his room, but then I want you to leave,' she stated, controlling the tremble in her voice with difficulty. 'Follow me.'

She led the way up and along the top corridor. Davey's music was seeping out from under his door as usual and

Lucille stopped mid-step, like a thoroughbred horse scenting the air. It was a plaintive Celtic lament which pierced to the very bones with its bittersweet melody. Davey's musical tastes were eclectic, to say the least, and Avril hoped that he wasn't attempting to emulate the lament in another song for the unappreciative Peggy.

As they approached, his door opened and Davey slouched out, his dark brown hair as wild as a poet's. He saw Lucille and smiled politely before passing them and clattering downstairs. Lucille's stare followed him briefly before she returned her attention to Avril.

Together they went into Gordon's neat lodgings. His casual jacket hung from his chair and the desk was lined with books. Avril felt a tenderness for him when she thought of him bent over the desk studying and marking jotters with dedication. She touched his jacket as if it were him. Lucille went round the room picking up

232

objects and setting them down. She looked out of the window and was unimpressed by the view. Then her eyes widened and she reached up to a high shelf of the bookcase.

'My letters.'

Was it at that moment that Avril's confidence crumbled? Gordon received so many letters, one a day, plus calls. Who else would contact him so frequently if not a lover? Why had it never sunk in before?

'I can prove I'm Gordon's fiancée,' Lucille was saying.

You don't need to! Avril wanted to shout. She bit down hard on her lip and tasted sour metal as it bled.

'Here we are, read this one,' Lucille said chattily, as if she was a friend sharing good news.

Numbly Avril took the proffered letter.

Dear Gordon
I am missing you terribly. The weather here is wet and windy, not

like Spring at all. I went to the witch's pond today and walked round it, thinking of you. Do you remember playing there as children? Ronnie made a model boat one summer, when you were both ten and I was eight. You'll know the one I mean — it had a red sail made from your father's scarf. You lived in fear of him finding out you'd 'borrowed' it.

What fun we had with that boat. We played with it for weeks until it snagged on a submerged branch and sank.

Take care, and call me soon.

I remain, as always, your loving Lucille.

★ ★ ★

The letter was embellished on the bottom with girlish crosses symbolising kisses.

Avril let it flutter from her hand. It floated down erratically to land on Lucille's shoe. She stooped to pick it up and while she did so, Avril ran from the room. Her vision was blurred with tears as she ran along the corridor. The sound of Gloria and Shirley's happy giggling clashed with her sobbing as she went, not knowing where she was going to — only that she was going away from Lucille and the letters and Gordon's betrayal.

* * *

She was half way to the allotment when she halted. It was her safe haven, but right now she couldn't bear to face Dad and have to tell him why she was crying. He was so very fond of Gordon, treating him like a second son. It would cut him to the core to find out he wasn't the honourable young man he'd believed in. Avril couldn't do that to her father.

She turned in the opposite direction, to the riverside path. Taking her handkerchief, she blotted her eyes and blew her nose and hoped she looked presentable, should she meet anyone. She needed to walk.

How she would face Gordon that evening she had no idea. As for Lucille, she never wanted to set eyes on her again. Gordon's behaviour wasn't her fault, but there was something about her that Avril could not like.

She walked swiftly along the path, not seeing the flowers or the butterflies flitting between them. Much further on, she saw a man walking towards her. As he got closer, she saw it was Jack. He was talking to himself and he was startled into a jump when he saw Avril.

'I was just thinking about you!' he exclaimed with pleasure. 'Having a conversation with you in my head, actually.'

Avril was too distracted to think this odd. Luckily Jack was too absorbed in his own musings to notice her distress. He kicked one shiny pointed toe against the other, leaving a dusty mark, and coughed. His face was high with colour and blotchy. Avril wondered briefly whether he was ill.

'What are you doing here, Jack? Aren't you meant to be on your way to London?'

'That's sort of why I'm here.' He coughed heartily and looked at his feet.

Avril didn't care. She wanted to be alone to sorrow in private. Impatiently she tapped her foot. If only Jack would move out of the way on the path, she could stride on. But he didn't budge. Instead he shoved his hands deep into his jacket pockets and looked at her.

'I want you to come with me, Avril. Come to London. I . . . I love you.' The words tumbled out of him.

There was a shocked silence. Avril's foot stilled.

'What are you suggesting?'

Jack stared out at the great cargo ships and their attendant tug boats as if fascinated. 'Let's get married,' he mumbled.

'What?'

'I said, let's get married,' he repeated with more confidence. 'Gretna Green's on the journey. Very romantic place and all that. And London's exciting. You'll see the Coronation, the new Queen. Living history, ain't it? You can have a bigger life than this place, Avril. Just say yes!'

Right now, she couldn't utter a single word, she was so astonished. Jack Lafferty had proposed to her — even if it was in an odd, roundabout way.

Her first instinct was to say no. She didn't love him, and it was madness to think she could uproot herself just like that. But as she stood there, Peggy's words came back to her.

You could do worse. Jack's fun. Jack's well-heeled. Jack likes you a lot. You could do worse.

In her anger and raw pain, it was suddenly a solution. If she left with Jack that afternoon, she need never face Gordon at all. She would never recover from the heartbreak, but maybe in London she could escape herself.

Jack was waiting for her reply. She didn't love him, there were no sparks between them — but he was a possible answer to her current problems.

She took a step towards him. 'Yes, I will marry you — but on one condition.'

'Which is?' Jack asked eagerly.

'That we leave right away. I don't want to spend another night under the boarding house roof.'

Jack was surprised and pleased, and agreed wholeheartedly. It fitted perfectly with his own plans, he told her. They arranged a time an hour hence so that they could gather their belongings. The rest could be sent later by courier, Jack said.

He took the liberty of kissing Avril lightly on the lips to seal their pact. Avril wanted to cry, but made herself smile at her fiancé. The kiss was soulless and meaningless. It left her cold, but she could hardly hurt Jack by confessing that.

Only one man could make her nerve endings tingle and ignite a fire within her. And he belonged to someone else.

13

'It's so romantic,' Peggy breathed. She took her white party shoes from her wardrobe and gave them to Avril. 'Here, I want you to have these. No arguments, okay? You won't have a wedding dress but you can at least look stylish.'

Avril's tears started up again. She took the shoes gratefully. She couldn't believe she was going through with this.

'Right, let's have a look in here for a suitable dress.' Peggy warmed to her task. 'Hmmm, what about my pastel green one?'

No — too many memories of the violence at the dance hall. Peggy must have realised it at the same moment because she moved on, picking out a white summer dress with crimson poppies on it.

'This is it. You'll make a beautiful

bride in this and it'll match the shoes perfectly. I've even got a white cardigan to go over it. I wish I could see you getting married,' she added wistfully.

'I wish you could, too,' Avril murmured, then rallied her resolve. 'We'll come back to Glasgow for a visit, remember? We won't lose touch, Peggy. I won't allow it.'

But it wouldn't be the same as living next door to each other and chatting every day. When would she and Jack return? She had no idea.

'I'll miss you so much,' Peggy wailed.

'Please don't cry, you'll set me off again,' Avril begged. She felt as if she'd wept a lake today and her head was pounding from it. 'Thank you for the clothes. I'll post them back to you when I get there. Remember, Peggy, it's a secret. You can't tell anyone that Jack and I are eloping.'

'I don't understand. I thought you were in love with Gordon. What's changed? If you waited, he'd come round to the idea. Wouldn't that be better than running off with Jack?'

'I don't want to talk about Gordon. Now promise me, Peggy, you won't tell anyone,' Avril demanded harshly.

Peggy nodded. 'I promise. I won't say a word. Oh — but your Mum's going to be so upset when she finds out. The Coronation street party's tomorrow. Can't you wait a while, Avril? Just until the party's over — and then go if you must. It won't be much of a celebration with you missing.'

'I can't stay, Peggy. I can't explain to you why, but I have to go this afternoon. I feel terrible missing the street party, but there's nothing I can do. Jack's keen to leave today, too. The worst part of it is leaving my family without telling them. So I've decided I'll stop on the way south and find a phone box and I'll ring them up and try to explain. I'll make them understand.'

Peggy gave her the bundle of clothes and they hugged.

'Good luck,' Peggy whispered.

＊　＊　＊

There was a frenzy of activity going on at the boarding house. Avril went in, noticing every detail and seeing her home as if for the last time. When would she be back again? Would Jack ever be welcome here after stealing Avril away to a secret wedding and a new life so far away? She could only hope and pray that her parents would forgive her in time.

There was a hubbub of noise coming from the open kitchen. Mrs Manderley, the butcher's wife, came out with a tray of steaming hot meat pies. The savoury aroma was delicious. Gloria and Shirley were skipping along following her, each with a pie to sample. Avril's temptation was to grab her little sisters and hug them tightly. She'd miss them so much.

'These are great. You should try one,' Gloria shouted to her as she disappeared up the road behind the butcher's wife.

'Avril, the lady's gone,' Shirley said

suddenly, a memory triggered. 'She said to tell you she'll be back later tonight.'

Later tonight Avril would be travelling far south of here. Lucille could do what she liked as far as Avril was concerned. It wouldn't change the facts nor the consequences. It simply hardened her resolve to go.

'Shirley,' she called. Shirley turned back, the pie safely consumed and only a moustache of flaky pastry left as evidence of its existence. Avril put her arms round her and hugged her tightly, smelling her clean hair and breathing in her warm scent of family.

'I love you,' she said, 'Tell Gloria I love her too.'

'You're a nutty noo.' Shirley wriggled free, embarrassed for Avril. She was too big to be babied these days by her elder sister. She ran off in search of Gloria.

Avril wanted to laugh and cry at the same time. She glanced at her watch. She was due to meet Jack in ten minutes. She had to hurry.

Inside the kitchen, there were far too

many cooks. Linda Garnett was yelling instructions over the hissing and bubbling of pots on the stove and the chatter of the other ladies. Her mother had the biggest kitchen in the street, so it was a natural place to congregate and co-ordinate the food for the party. Avril saw six neighbourhood wives exchanging comments and tips. Even old Mrs Petrocelli was there, up to her elbows in dough and flour while Mrs Peck from four doors down bossed her about. As she was double the width of Mrs Petrocelli, the old lady was doing what she was told. Avril could tell she was secretly enjoying it.

Linda caught sight of her. 'Avril, where have you been? You need to take Dad his lunch. He'll be so cross, I forgot about it and it's over an hour late. Then I'll need you to bake Victoria sponges. I was telling Mrs Peck what a good baker you are. Your cakes rise better than my own.'

There was a note of real pride in her mother's voice. At once, a lump stuck in Avril's throat. She couldn't leave them.

But she had to! She couldn't bear to stay. She took the sandwiches in their familiar crease of greaseproof paper.

'The street party's going to be a wonderful success, Mum, and it's all down to you,' she declared with conviction.

'Nonsense, love. I've had lots of willing helpers.' But she looked pleased.

Avril kissed her on the cheek.

'What's all that for? Get along with you and don't forget those sandwiches,' Linda said, pretending to be stern. But when Avril had gone, she touched her cheek and smiled.

Avril couldn't go to the allotment. She just couldn't. It would be better to call later from the roadside. If she saw Dad now, she'd tell him everything. It would gush forth like a river undammed. Instead she went up to Davey's room.

'Will you take Dad his lunch, Davey? No excuses, for once — please just do

246

it,' she said. Then she paused. 'Why aren't you at work?'

Davey laid aside his guitar and the piece of paper he was scribbling music onto. 'I lost my job. I was off ill too much so they sacked me.'

Avril was appalled. She'd been so caught up in her own problems, she hadn't noticed Davey's.

'That's so awful. What are you going to do?'

Davey shrugged. 'I was expecting it, to be honest. The manager's son needed work and had his eye on my clerk's position. I'm not daft, I could see he was working out how to get rid of me.'

'You have to do something! That's outrageous.'

Davey gave a soft laugh. 'You take things too much to heart, Avril. Life's easier if you go with the flow, believe me. I'll be fine, I'll find a job, it'll come to me.'

She did take things to heart, that was true. Her very flight south today was proof of that. But she wasn't capable of being otherwise. It would not be fine to stay and be eaten up with bitterness and jealousy watching Gordon with Lucille.

'That girl knocked on my door after you left earlier,' Davey remarked.

'What did she want?'

He took up his guitar and strummed lightly on it. He was happiest when he played it.

'She cried,' he said simply.

Avril didn't want to feel sympathy for Lucille but she couldn't help it. The poor young woman.

'Why did she cry?'

What on earth did she have to cry about? She had Gordon, didn't she!

'I didn't ask,' Davey said, adding with the logic of a young man, 'I played her music, all sorts, and it soothed her. I even played some of my own compositions. She really liked them. She knows lots about music and she plays the clarsach.'

'I've got to go now. I'll see you soon.'

Davey gave her a weird look. 'Yeah, at

dinner time. What's got into you? You're acting a bit strange.'

'I'm not feeling too good. I might go and lie down for a while,' Avril lied. 'Actually can you tell Mum I can't bake this afternoon and ask everyone not to disturb me?'

That should give her and Jack a very reasonable head start.

★ ★ ★

Jack's car was parked several streets away. Avril lugged her suitcase along the road. She was pretty sure she'd escaped unnoticed out of the little-used side door of the house. To be honest, everyone was far too interested in the next day's party to notice anything else. Jack was there, packing up the back of the car with too many cases and boxes when she arrived.

'Hello darling,' he said, half jokingly, as if they were already a married couple. He leaned forward to kiss her and Avril jerked back involuntarily.

'I am going to be your husband very soon,' Jack said reproachfully. He reached for her again and Avril let him.

'I'm sorry, it's not you. It's me. I'm sad to be leaving,' she said, mixing a lie with the truth. She was going to become good at lying, if she didn't watch out. Come to think of it, she had a lifetime of lies ahead of her. Her marriage to Jack would be the biggest lie of all.

Put a bit of effort in, will you, she told herself. So she took the initiative and pressed her lips to Jack's. He held her shoulders and returned it eagerly. He was obviously enjoying it but Avril wasn't. She used the pretext of packing her case to move away from him.

'Let's get this in somehow. Then we should go.'

'Let me, my darling. It's quite light. Are you sure you've packed enough clothing?'

'I think so. I can buy more when we get to London, if not.'

Jack looked doubtful. 'We won't have

much cash at first. You'll have to make do and mend, as me old granny used to say.' He grinned.

'I thought . . . you've got a car and nice clothes. I thought you were well off.' Avril felt a twinge of uncertainty. How would they manage if Jack had no money?

'I've had a little dip in my finances,' he admitted, glancing about as if someone might hear. 'But it's temporary. Once we get to London, we'll be all right, you'll see. My fortunes are about to change.'

She wasn't sure what he meant by that but a wave of tiredness suddenly hit her. She sank back into the passenger seat of the car and closed her eyes. She'd made her choice, and now had to live with the consequences.

It was too bad that she was missing Gordon already. She could cry all she liked but it wouldn't bring him back.

As they drove away, another car slid smoothly onto the road and followed them.

14

He had to see Avril. Gordon strode along the pavement with purpose. His limp was barely noticeable and his leg didn't hurt. A year of healing was up. Today in the classroom he'd had a revelation. It was such a powerful one that he'd actually left the pupils with another teacher, feigning sickness, something he had never ever done before in his teaching career. Now he had to get home.

He hurried, desperate to make things right. The thaw that had started with Avril's delightful friendship was complete. He was alive again. It had struck him as a blow. He loved Avril, and she loved him. There was no barrier between them except of his own creation. He alone had the power to dissolve it. He chose now to do so.

Ronnie's presence was gently fading.

The agony he committed himself to every day was less and less raw. A year had passed since the accident and, without noticing, he was gradually coming to terms with it. He had blamed himself, but he was learning to forgive himself.

Telling Avril and hearing her views on the terrible events had helped beyond belief. Gordon felt like a new man. One who could love and be loved. One who deserved happiness. Avril's kiss had melted the last obstacle. It was like a glacier breaking off into the ocean, releasing a torrential river behind it.

His love flowed out to her. Yes, he'd resisted it. He'd told himself he wasn't ready. He'd told her it could never work. He had been frightened, that was all. But today in class, it came to him. He didn't need to be afraid. With Avril at his side, he had the power to make a new and loving life ahead. New starts were all around. Spring itself was a burst of new life. The Coronation of the new young Queen was that start of a bright new reign that could span the decades. He'd never felt this good.

He took a detour from the road and went down to the river path. The water still repulsed him. There was still dread associated with it. Perhaps there always would be.

'I'm going to ask her to marry me,' he announced. There was no answer, of course.

He went on to the boarding house. There were lots of people going in and out and the smell of cooking and the ring of hammering. Aline Street was going to put on the best party ever.

Gordon dodged everyone, looking impatiently for Avril. He spotted Davey in the throng, munching on a stolen bun.

'Where's Avril?' he asked.

'She's lying down for a bit. She's asked not to be disturbed,' Davey mumbled through a mouthful of sponge.

Gordon's disappointment was acute.

He would have to wait.

'There's a note for you from your friend,' Davey added helpfully. He delved into his pocket and came up with a piece of paper and gave it to Gordon. Frowning, he scanned it.

It was from Lucille. She had made good on her threat to visit, and had arrived. She wanted to meet him and gave the name of a restaurant where she could be found all afternoon.

Lucille was quite capable of sitting for hours on one place if she had music to listen to. Gordon didn't want to see her, but he had to. He had to persuade her to go home. To start living again, the way he intended to.

* * *

Lucille was sitting in a corner booth, nursing a small cup of black coffee. The remains of an iced biscuit were scattered on a china plate in front of her.

Gordon slid into the seat opposite.

255

'Hello, Lucille.'

'Gordon — you came for me.' There was relief but also certainty in her voice.

'I got your note,' he replied, non-committally.

'I've missed you so much,' Lucille murmured. 'But I'm here now. We don't have to be apart any more.'

'Do your parents know you've come to Glasgow?'

Lucille shook her head impatiently. 'They nag, nag, nag. They can't leave me alone. They want me to get a job, to find a boyfriend — to go out dancing. They just don't understand. I've got you . . .'

Gordon ordered a coffee from the waitress hovering nearby. He didn't want their conversation to be overheard. Lucille could be very intense.

'But I'm not your boyfriend, Lucille,' he said carefully. 'Your parents are right. You need to start living again.'

'What about the letters and the calls?' she asked, her voice rising. A couple

256

glanced over at them and she lowered it. 'Did they mean nothing to you?'

'They mean a lot. We've been two friends helping each other over a great loss. But not more than that. You think you love me, Lucille, but you don't. I'm an anchor — a safe harbour for you. It's a brotherly love.'

Her pale eyes flashed brightly and she hissed, 'You love her, don't you? The girl at the boarding house. That's why you're saying this.'

'Her? If you mean Avril, then yes. I'm in love with her. I'm intending to marry her and I very much hope you'll wish us well.'

'It won't work, you know,' Lucille retorted, her face ugly with triumph. 'I told her I was your fiancée. I showed her my letters as proof and she believed me. Well, there were so many letters. I could see she thought you must have answered just as many. Only lovers could exchange letters so fast. I'm as good as your fiancée, aren't I? I've waited for you these long years,

Gordon. You won't find her so constant.'

Gordon stood up, his knuckles white. 'You did what?'

She shrank from his fury.

'I have told you many times. I don't love you and I never will. If you can't accept that, Lucille, then I never want to see you or hear from you again!'

He threw on his jacket, incensed by her doggedness.

'Wait!' Lucille cried. She ran after him, leaving the waitress nonplussed, holding the ordered cup of coffee.

Outside, she called out, 'Gordon, wait please.'

He clamped down on his jaw and turned back to her. She was a striking woman, tall and strong with dramatic Celtic colouring. He felt overwhelmingly that it was a great pity she'd wasted years on him, instead of seeking out a soulmate of her own.

'I'm sorry.'

How strange the effect two little

words could have. Gordon's fury left him. Lucille was redeemable. Her long red hair whipped in the wind like flames on a fire.

'I can't never see you. I don't want to lose you as well as Ronnie,' she whispered.

'You won't lose me. But you have to let go. I'm in love with Avril. I can't offer you anything but friendship. That's all I've ever offered you. Why can't it be enough?'

She stood immobile, taking it in. Really taking it in for the first time. Then she was moving with him, saying, 'You have to find her. She was very upset — she may have gone.'

They reached the open boarding house. Gordon took the stairs two at a time, uncaring of his leg. He rapped on Avril's door loudly. There was silence. He pushed it open; her room was empty. Avril was gone.

'Try the kitchen. She's probably helping Mum,' Davey said helpfully from behind him. When he turned

Lucille was there too, and their gazes locked.

Gordon knew Avril would not be in the house. His anger at Lucille had gone. He would not trouble with the past. The future was what mattered.

He left Lucille with Davey. There was one person who would know where Avril was . . . Gordon went to find Peggy.

15

Peggy looked terrified when she saw Gordon. She pressed her lips together as if to stop herself talking.

'Where is she?' Gordon asked. 'Please, Peggy — I have to find her.'

'I don't know,' Peggy muttered, rubbing an earlobe and not meeting his eyes.

Gordon sighed. 'I know you're lying. You're just trying to protect her I understand that, but I must speak to her. Where has she gone?'

Peggy groaned. 'It's a secret. She made me promise not to tell anyone.'

Now Gordon was getting worried. He'd imagined Avril was angry with him at his supposed deception of her with Lucille. He thought she might have stormed over to Peggy's house or gone for a long walk by the river. But she'd made Peggy promise not to tell where she was. She didn't want him to find her.

'If you really are her best friend and care about her, then you'll tell me,' Gordon said insistently.

'Why?' Peggy demanded. 'Why should I tell you? You've hurt her. Avril refused to talk about you and she was very upset when she left. I was sure she was making a bad decision, but she's made up her mind.'

'What bad decision? Where is she?' Gordon felt a great desire to shake the truth out of Peggy.

'She loves you.' Peggy shook her head. 'I don't know what you did, but you've ruined it.'

Gordon rubbed his face wearily. 'It is my fault, you're right. I should've told her how I feel and that I love her too. Instead I've let her slip away. But that's why I need to find her now. I have to tell her that I love her.'

'Oh!' Peggy's face brightened in a wide smile. 'So you do care about her after all.' Then her brows drew in. 'But you're too late. She's marrying Jack Lafferty.'

'What!' The blood drained from Gordon's face.

The whole story fell from Peggy's lips in a rush. She was useless at keeping secrets and it was a relief to let it all out. When she was done, Gordon stood still for a moment.

'That lowlife, good for nothing . . . he's not going to marry Avril. He's going to ruin her.'

'But they're going to Gretna Green. It's very romantic,' Peggy protested. 'It's on the way to London,' she added helpfully.

'When did they say they were intending to arrive in London?' Gordon asked.

Peggy looked surprised. 'Well — very late tonight I should think or early morning. It's a long journey, but they were only making the one stop. You can get married there very fast.'

'Not that quickly,' Gordon told her, already on his way out. 'Jack will know, as I do, that you have to be resident for at least three weeks in Gretna before you can marry there. He's lied to Avril and he's stolen her away.'

Peggy started to cry. 'Bring her back, Gordon! Please bring her back safely.'

'I intend to,' he said grimly. 'Whatever it takes.'

David Garnett was leaning over the allotment gate when Gordon arrived. He took one look at Gordon's thunderous expression and stood up straight.

'What's up?'

'David, you've been like a father to me since I arrived,' Gordon said seriously. 'I've appreciated hearing the stories about my own father and I've learned to know him better. I need your help again now on a different matter. It's Avril.'

'Is she all right?' David asked, alarmed.

'She will be,' Gordon answered. 'But she's . . . she's run away and it's all my fault. I have to go after her and bring her home safely.'

'Her mother mustn't find out,' David Garnett said immediately. 'Is she alone? Do you know where she's gone?'

'I know where she's going, yes — and I can bring her back safely before anyone need know a thing about it. But I need a favour from you.'

'My car?'

It was David Garnett's pride and joy. Rarely driven but polished lovingly every day, it lived in a garage at the end of the street. In fact, Gordon had often helped David to tinker with it in the evenings.

'Can you drive it? Your leg?'

'I can drive it,' Gordon declared. He'd have to — it was as simple as that. Though it wasn't the physical problem of using his damaged leg that was his concern; it was the fact that he hadn't been in a car since the accident.

'Come on, then. Let's go and get it running.'

They walked together the short distance to the garage, where David gave him the key. He paused.

'You love my daughter, don't you?'

'Yes.'

'Look after her. You don't have to tell me who she's run off with. Just remember this. Avril can be impulsive and she's made a mistake, but she has a good heart. If she loves you, you won't find a better companion in life.'

'There's nothing to forgive. It's I who must apologise to her.'

The older man grasped Gordon's hand in an unspoken blessing. Touched, Gordon turned to the car. A cold sweat broke on his forehead as he slid into the driver's seat. He gripped the steering wheel. Flashes of memories of his last drive with Ronnie surfaced. He pushed them down.

Avril. He must think only of her. He had to rescue her. To do so, he needed this car.

He took one deep breath, then another. They steadied him. Slowly his concentration returned. He looked out of the windscreen, towards the open road.

David Garnett stood patiently to the side of the garage waiting for him to leave. He turned the ignition; the engine roared. He put the car into gear and it moved forwards. His leg felt strong.

The car crawled out on to the road and David lifted his hand in a wave. Gordon returned the gesture. He put his foot down and the vehicle's speed increased. The Tarmac was eaten up under him. He was driving.

It didn't feel good or comfortable or safe, but as he took the first corner he knew he didn't need those feelings. All he needed for his mission were a near-empty road, no diversions — and a burning fury at Jack Lafferty.

16

Avril yawned and stretched as much as she could in the confines of the passenger seat. She'd fallen asleep as they left the city, but she felt better for it. She looked out the window with interest. They were no longer boxed in by tenements and towering blocks of blackened buildings. Now they passed neat little houses with gardens, a town square decked in red, white and blue flags for the next day and a stables where glossy, groomed horses leaned over the fence to watch them go by.

'Where are we?' she asked Jack.

'Out of Glasgow at least,' he said cheerfully. 'Into the back end of nowhere.'

'It's not that bad,' Avril protested. 'I think it's quite pretty actually. I could picture myself living somewhere like this when I'm older.'

'Not me.' Jack shuddered in distaste. 'I'd die in a hole like this. It's got to be the city where there's lots happening. All hustle and bustle. Didn't you want excitement?'

'Yes,' she admitted. 'But I've come to see that there are other ways of finding it. My writing for example, excites me.'

Jack made a noise. Avril ignored it, pursuing the conversation. 'Couldn't we live in a small town when we're an old married couple? We could have a big white house with a garden. Maybe an apple tree and a pond for the children to play by.'

'Children? You're joking.' Jack sounded alarmed. 'I can't stand children.'

There was a gulf between them on many issues, Avril thought with a sinking heart. Why had they never discussed topics like these? The irony of it was, she was finally getting to know Jack when it was too late to decide whether they were compatible.

She looked down at herself. Peggy's lovely dress was crumpled from the journey already. She smoothed it down. The poppies cheered her up. She must make this work with Jack. There was no alternative.

'I'm looking forward to meeting your father,' she said as brightly as she could.

'He won't be too happy to see you,' Jack said, glancing over from his driving.

'Why ever not?' Avril buttoned up her soft, white cardigan against a sudden chill.

'Extra mouth to feed.' Jack laughed. It wasn't a kind sound.

She shrank down onto the seat feeling lost and lonely. What had she ever seen in Jack Lafferty? She cursed her wish for excitement. Look what it had brought her. Hadn't she had it all? A loving family around her, a solid comfortable home to live in and good food to eat. She remembered her father's proud words about her mother providing for them all. That's what she wanted. It would be enough for her. To create a happy family of her own with a man she loved.

Now none of that would happen. Tears welled up and she brushed them away angrily. It was all her own fault. She should have waited for Gordon and let him explain about Lucille. She was sure he loved her. That kiss had pulled away their defences. Their naked emotions had shown. He couldn't possibly have faked those.

Now she had wrecked everything. It was too late for her. If Gordon found out where she was and who she was with, he'd be disgusted with her. That she could so easily go off with another man. He might even believe she loved Jack! He'd seen them together. It wasn't inconceivable. He would turn his back on her. Even if he hadn't loved Lucille before, would Avril's actions send him running into her oh-so-willing arms?

She would not cry! She stared despairingly out the window. They were about to enter a village. There was a red telephone kiosk next to the village's name board.

'Oh stop, please,' she cried. 'I need to phone home. I have to tell my family that I'm safe.'

'Now?' Jack demanded impatiently. 'Can't it wait? You can tell them when we get to London, surely.'

'But that won't be until the morning, will it? They'll be frantic if I don't appear for dinner and they'll have the police out if I'm not in my bed tonight.'

The word 'police' did the trick. Jack roughly pulled the car off onto the side of the road, leaving the engine running.

'Hurry up, then, will you? One quick call, that's it. No long girly gossip.'

Avril was glad to stretch her legs. The air smelt of dirty-sweet hawthorn blossom, cattle and exhaust fumes, but it was lovely to be outside. She went into the kiosk and dialled eagerly. It rang. She looked about. There were rolling fields stretching out to the horizon on one side of the village. Cows and sheep were dotted about, little blots of white and brown and black. A tractor chugged across the crest of a nearby hill followed by a flock of calling crows. There was another car on the road coming towards the village. It was shiny black with darkened glass so she couldn't see the occupants. It glided on a quiet engine past the kiosk.

The phone rang out. Where was everyone? Avril was panicky. Jack might not let her stop again. Then, with relief, she thought there was bound to be a telephone at Gretna. Could she slip away from her own wedding to phone?

There was a sharp, impatient rap on the glass.

'What's taking you so long? We have to go.' Jack's fleshy face was ruddy with annoyance.

Reluctantly Avril put down the receiver. It clicked with a depressing finality.

★   ★   ★

They drove on monotonously. After a while even Avril was fed up of little villages and green fields and hedgerows.

273

Jack kept adjusting the mirror and glancing out of the car, making it swerve terribly. After a near miss with a horse and cart, Avril couldn't contain herself.

'What are you doing, Jack? You nearly killed us there. What are you looking for?'

'Nothing. Nothing.' He began to hum tunelessly.

Avril gritted her teeth. She was ready to kill him herself. How many more hours of this could she endure before they reached Gretna Green?

She looked back over her shoulder trying to see what he was looking at. There was nothing out of the ordinary. The open road behind them, flanked by tall trees and open grasslands. A black car appeared on the distant curve and she squinted at it.

'That's strange. I'm sure that's the same car that passed us in the village. How did it get behind us, Jack? Jack!'

Jack had stopped humming. His grip on the steering wheel was tight. There were beads of moisture on his brow and his oiled hair was out of place.

'Do you know that car?' Avril persisted.

'We need to keep going,' Jack murmured, more to himself than to her.

'Jack, answer me. Who are they? What do they want?' Avril suppressed a shiver of fear. It couldn't be anything too bad, surely. Maybe it was a coincidence. This was the main route south, after all.

Just as she had this comforting thought, Jack suddenly swung the steering wheel round and the car veered off left down a narrow country lane, taking a chunk of hedgerow with it.

'Careful! What are you doing? This isn't the way.' Avril screamed. A great, leafy branch obscured her door until it dropped away as Jack sped up.

'Shut up,' he snarled. 'I know what I'm doing. It's a detour. We can rejoin the main route further on.'

Avril was shaken; she'd never heard him speak so harshly before. She sat in silence. The lane was rutted and unsurfaced in places and the car bounced and crunched over it. A desolate grey farmhouse stood in a field. The derelict windows were like bleak eyes as they drove past.

'I'm sorry,' Jack said, trying to grin at her. 'I shouldn't have lost it with you back there. It's the driving, it gets to me. Pity you can't drive, we could share it.'

'I'd like to learn one day,' Avril said, making an effort to sound normal. Ahead of them the landscape changed to flattened brown earth fields. A huddle of old outhouses stood like trolls in the distance. In front of them, snaking along, was a deep-sided man-made canal. Avril wound down the window and the air seeped in, thick with a bacterial soil and algal stench.

'What a horrible place,' she said. 'Where have all the pretty villages disappeared to?'

Jack's head jerked and she followed his gaze.

Over to the right, on a higher

gradient than their own road, ran the main route south. With a chill, Avril saw it. A black car easing along it, keeping pace with them.

'Who are they?' she whispered in horror.

Jack looked at her, then back to the road. 'We'll be okay as long as we keep moving. I can lose them south of here when it gets built up. But we can't stop. Do you understand?'

'But what about Gretna Green? We have to get married.' She heard the tremble in her voice and wasn't quite certain if it was fear or anger.

'We can't stop,' Jack repeated forcefully.

'But we have to get married,' Avril's voice rose. 'Today.'

'Look, Avril. Even if we did stop at Gretna, they wouldn't marry us today.'

'What are you saying? You said we were going to get married. I can't just go off with you otherwise.'

'You're not that kind of girl,' Jack finished for her, a hint of a sneer under the surface. Their car was curving round now. The canal was close, with the huddle of broken buildings beyond. Soon the lane would join up again with the main road. At the junction, high above them, the black car idled.

'You have to stay in Gretna for three weeks before you can get married.' Jack was talking fast now, his eye fixed firmly on the car above.

'You were never going to marry me,' Avril whispered rawly. Her throat closed over painfully and she swallowed.

'It's only a piece of paper,' Jack protested. 'We'd still be happy. You've no idea how badly I want you, Avril.'

'You want me but you don't love me,' Avril said shakily. 'How could you do this, Jack? If you cared for me at all?'

'I do care for you. I'll make it up to you, I promise.'

'Tell me who's in the black car.' Avril was suddenly deadly calm. A numbness enveloped her.

'I owe money to people,' Jack muttered.

'The two men who came into the cafe?' she guessed.

Jack nodded. His eyes flicked nervously to the road junction.

'Why don't you pay them?'

'I haven't got it, have I? That's why we have to get to London. Don't you see? — it'll be okay. I'll make the money and we can have a good life. We don't need marriage, you and I. There'll be plenty of excitement.'

'I don't want excitement with you, Jack Lafferty. Stop the car; I want to get out!' Avril said.

'I can't stop the car.'

The car had slowed for the curve. Avril knew what she had to do. She pulled the handle and the door opened. Ignoring Jack's shout, she jumped and fell onto the grassy verge. Before he could react, Avril was up and running.

She didn't have a plan. Her only instinct was to get away from Jack.

Before her was the canal, then the farm outhouses. She made for the buildings. She ran raggedly, her breath coming fast and uneven. Glancing round, she saw Jack get out of the car, half running towards her. The black car eased down onto the lane and purred towards him. Jack was caught in the middle. Avril slipped in the sticky mud and one of Peggy's white shoes came off. She left it swamped and went on. The stink of the mud clogged her nostrils. Now she was on the steep concrete slope of the canal. She had to cross it to get to the buildings. She took a last look at Jack. His arms were outstretched to her. But the black car had almost reached him. He called her name one last time. Then Jack ran back to his own car and high-tailed it back along the lane with the black car in pursuit.

Sobbing, Avril teetered on the edge of the canal. Her poppy dress was smeared with black mud and her bare foot was bleeding. She sat on the edge. The concrete was rough and unyielding. There was no bridge. With a sigh, she slid down to the water. She could swim across to shelter, she reasoned hazily. She stepped into the cold water. It sucked her in greedily. The weight of her clothing leadened and Avril was tugged away from the concrete lip like a child plucked by a parent's grip.

'Gordon — help!' she screamed. It was futile. She had to struggle. She couldn't die here. It couldn't end like this. Avril fought the water, but it was deep and thick and full of low currents. She was moving now as part of it. Her hands scrabbled uselessly at the steep sides.

⋆ ⋆ ⋆

Gordon had eaten up the miles. Luckily there were few other cars on the roads. His nerves had steadied and he was able to keep the car moving smoothly south. Peggy had described Jack's car to him and he looked about as much as he could on the way, desperate not to miss them. They could have stopped anywhere along the route, but he guessed that Jack would want to keep moving.

He passed a pretty village with a red telephone kiosk and wondered whether Avril had phoned home. He hoped not. He'd promised her father he'd bring her home safe and sound before her mother found out. There was no need for the incident to be uncovered if he intercepted them in time. He reckoned Avril and he could be back by late night.

Peggy had promised to give them an alibi. It was an unlikely one, but all she could come up with at such short notice. If Linda Garnett wondered where her daughter was, she was staying at Peggy's, making Coronation Day decorations. Peggy was already hard at work with glue and paper, creating the evidence.

As for Jack Lafferty . . . when Gordon caught up with him, he didn't know how he would react. A murderous rage rose in him when he thought of Jack.

He slammed on the brakes. A road branched off left from the main road. He would've driven right past it but for the damaged hedgerow. Someone had driven a car at speed right through it.

A gut instinct told him to turn down the lane. He'd drive along it for a bit. If he found nothing, he would rejoin the main road.

It was a barren landscape, Gordon thought. A great, flat plain smeared with mud. An old ruined farmhouse loomed out at him. Further along, he could see the outhouses and farm buildings belonging to it. He decided he would drive to the curve in the road. If there was no sign of another car, he'd go back and head south via the main route.

He drove along, seeing nothing. Avril and Jack were probably miles away by now. He wondered when Jack would tell her they couldn't marry. He throttled the steering wheel, wishing it was Jack Lafferty's neck.

He stopped the car, pulling off the verge just after the curve, and got out. There was silence apart from a soughing wind. It brought a stench with it. Gordon shivered. There was nothing here. He needed to go on; he'd follow them all the way to London if he had to.

He was already ducking his tall frame back into the car when he glimpsed it. Something white in the mud. Frowning, he leapt the ditch and stalked across the clinging mud to get it. It was a girl's shoe. A white, pretty one — the kind a girl might go dancing in. Or wear to her wedding.

Then he was shouting until his throat was raw, 'Avril! Avril! Where are you?' He ran as fast as he could through the soil to the edge of the canal. The water was dark and sinister. The concrete sides were steep and stained with dark green slime where the water had tasted the stonework.

Gordon's heart pounded. Where was she? *Please God, don't let her be in here*. He noticed a white piece of material further along, snagged on a branch. Then he saw it was her.

'Avril,' he shouted.

She raised her head with difficulty. 'Gordon? Is it really you? I'm okay. I'm holding the branch but I can't get up the side.'

'Don't worry, my darling. I'm coming to get you.'

Gordon's heart was singing now. He'd found her! She was his darling, there was no doubt about that. He wanted to yell *I love you*, but it could keep. First he had to get her out of there.

He sat on the rough edge of the canal. Fear rose like bile. He was re-living the horror of being trapped underwater in the river. It didn't matter. None of it mattered. He had to save Avril whatever the cost.

Gordon stretched out his legs and started the slide into the murky liquid.

The water pulled at him and he let it take him. Then, all at once, he heard Ronnie's voice in his mind, telling him it was going to be okay. A great peace descended on him.

'Ronnie, we have to save her,' Gordon said aloud. 'I couldn't save you and I'm sorry — but I can do this.'

Again Ronnie's comforting presence calmed him as the water soaked into him and he half swam and half crawled along the canalside towards his love.

Avril was tired, so very tired. Her arms were cramped from clinging to the branch. More flotsam and jetsam had gathered around her. She'd created a tiny whirlpool. It had mesmerised her for what seemed like hours. She'd tried to climb up the canalside but failed, sliding down to the branch again each time. Finally she hugged the hard wood and waited. She'd lost her other shoe and her feet were freezing. The dye in the poppies had bled, tainting the white cotton streaky pink.

Gordon was here. It was a dream, but

a very good one. Here he came now, swimming confidently towards her. The real Gordon couldn't do that.

'Peggy's going to be so mad. I've lost her shoes,' she told the Gordon mirage.

'I don't think she'll mind,' he soothed. 'She'll just be glad to see you're safe.'

'You feel very solid,' Avril told him, laughing sleepily. 'Warm, too. I'm so cold.'

'You have to help me,' Gordon urged. 'We have to get out of here. I can push you up the side as far as I can but you have to grab on and hoist yourself up. Can you do that?'

Avril nodded. 'I love you. I wish I'd told you better so you loved me back. I miss you.'

'I love you too, with all my heart,' Gordon said fervently. 'Now, let's go.'

He peeled her off the branch with difficulty and pushed her up the concrete side as far as possible. Avril stretched out her tired arms. Her fingertips found purchase on the lip.

They slid off. With a final burst of energy, Gordon gave her a shove. Avril shrieked but grabbed on. Then she was scrambling up with Gordon close behind. Heedless of the mud, she lay on the ground, looking up at the grey sky.

Gordon leaned over her and kissed her.

'It really is you,' she said wonderingly. 'How did you manage to find me?'

'Lucille told me what she'd done,' Gordon explained. 'I'm so sorry. She's not a bad person, but she's been mixed up for a long while. Then Peggy told me where you'd gone.'

'She can't keep a secret, poor Pegs.' Avril laughed, finishing on a wheeze.

Gordon hugged her tenderly. 'You're cold and soaked. We can talk later. Let's get you dried out and warmed up.'

But Avril put a gentle hand to his chest to stay him. 'I'm okay. I want to hear you say you love me again.'

'I love you,' he growled softly, catching her with a kiss that was deep and full of longing.

'I'm sorry I was so foolish,' Avril whispered, kissing him back. 'I should have trusted you. But Lucille was very convincing and when I saw her letter she showed me, I believed her. I was so hurt and angry, I took Jack's offer to run away. I was going to marry him and never have to see you and Lucille together, ever. Jack . . . ' She looked over at the road, remembering the two cars driving too fast along the lane.

'Forget him, he's not worth talking about,' Gordon said, gathering her to him. 'Let's talk about us instead. How would you feel about becoming Mrs Silver?'

'Mrs Silver.' Avril rolled it around in her mouth. 'It has such a lovely ring to it. Garnett to Silver. No longer a semi-precious stone but rather a precious metal. I think I'd feel very happy.'

Gordon wrapped his arms more tightly about her and kissed her cold forehead.

'You are very precious. But if we don't get you back up the road double-quick, there won't be a choice. It'll be a shot-gun wedding. It's getting late.'

Her face fell suddenly. 'Do Mum and Dad know that I went?'

Gordon shook his head. 'No-one knows except Peggy and your Dad — and he'll keep it quiet. I had to tell him to borrow the car, you see.'

'Won't they wonder where I am now?'

'No,' Gordon answered blithely. 'Because right now you're at Peggy's house making decorations in red, white and blue.'

'I am?'

'Most definitely,' he assured her.

Once they were in the car, and Avril was well wrapped up in a blanket Gordon had found in the boot, she thought of something.

'You swam in the canal to get me. It was you.'

'I had no choice.' Gordon started up the car and made the turn. 'I had to save you.'

He slowed down, letting the engine rumble. 'The most marvellous thing happened, Avril — Ronnie was with me. I felt him very clearly. He told me I could do it. I've finally forgiven myself, Avril. I can lay Ronnie to rest properly in my mind. I'll never forget him, but from now on my memories of him are going to be happy ones.'

'I'm so glad,' she cried, leaning into him tenderly. The car engine was allowed to tick over for quite a while due to Avril insisting on two more long kisses.

With a reluctant sigh, Gordon eventually took the steering wheel. 'Darling, we really must go, much as I'd like to kiss you like that all night.'

'Some sleep wouldn't go amiss.' Avril yawned. 'Especially as it's the Coronation tomorrow. We want to enjoy it. I can't wait to be home with Mum and Dad, Davey and the twins. And to see Peggy. And never, ever to be apart from you again, my darling Gordon.' She snuggled down under the blanket.

The sky had turned the most beautiful shades of turquoise and navy blue and a single star twinkled like a diamond. Gordon revved her father's car, and it speed along the lane, up on to the main road and in the direction of home.

17

They were all crowded into the front room until it was standing space only. Gloria squeezed Avril's hand excitedly. 'I can't believe Mum and Dad bought a television. Jessie at school's going to be sooo jealous.'

'You mustn't boast about it,' Avril chided, then relented because Gloria was shining with happiness. 'But you're right, it's fantastic we've got a television so we can see the Coronation as it happens. It's like magic.'

What was also magic, from Avril's point of view, was to be safely back at home, sitting on the couch squashed between Gloria and Shirley, feeling their warm bodies nestled against her. She loved them so much.

There was a sudden 'oooh' from the family and neighbours as they caught sight of the royal coach on its way to

Westminster Abbey. Mr Manderley, the butcher, was standing in front of them. He sat down heavily on the chair provided, but that proved to be worse as his round head and sticking-out ears obscured most of her view of the flickering screen. Avril leaned sideways in an attempt to see around him, only to be treated to more of Shirley's complaints.

'Am I late?' a man said and Avril's heart pounded happily.

Shirley complained again as Gordon manoeuvred in beside Avril. 'Why must you sit there? I'm stuck on the armrest now.'

She was soon quiet, eyes fixed on the procession, having realised she had a better vantage point with no one's head in the way. Avril was perfectly content with Gordon right there beside her.

They had arrived back in pitch darkness and sneaked in to the house. There was a lamp still on in the sitting room. David Garnett came out, looking tired but very relieved to see them.

'You made it,' he said softly.

Avril rushed into his arms with a stifled sob. 'I'm okay, Dad. Thanks to Gordon. I'm sorry I caused you to worry.'

He patted her back. 'We'll say no more about it.'

He turned to Gordon and said simply, 'Thank you.' But there was a wealth of emotion in the two words.

Gordon simply nodded. There was no need to say more. The two men understood each other perfectly. Then they were all heading upstairs.

Avril was ready to collapse from exhaustion. Once she had bathed and was warm and dry, her head hit the pillow and she was asleep instantly.

Gordon's sleep was full of dreams. He relived saving Avril. He drove along strange roads. Memories became dreams where he and Ronnie and Lucille ran with the lithe, endless energy of the young across the glens of his childhood. A great feeling of peace stole over him, and finally he slept deeply and dreamlessly until morning.

* * *

Much later in the day, the street party began. Avril thought that Aline Street had never looked so good. The weather, which had started off that morning damp and grey, had brightened. The trestle tables lined one section of the pavement. They were draped with white tablecloths and laden with plates of delicious food. Peggy's decorations enlivened the tables and were hung on the lamp posts too.

The men had put out chairs and smaller tables on the street, and blocked any access from cars with pieces of fencing from the allotment. Not that anyone would be driving today. Everyone was celebrating the momentous occasion.

Avril was looking for Gordon. He'd gone off with her father and Bert to place the garden furniture and fix a rickety table leg. She was bursting with joy.

'Look at this,' she cried when she found him.

Gordon took the letter from her. A grin broke across his face.

'That's wonderful — well done. You deserve it. I knew you could do it.' He swung her up in a hug that swirled her round and made her squeal. Linda Garnett saw it and was startled. Then she smiled contentedly and returned to her task of ladling her Coronation Chicken into serving bowls.

'I can't believe they want to publish my article in a real magazine.' Avril shook her head.

'You could write more,' Gordon encouraged. 'There are lots of topics to cover — in fact, you've got a lifetime of writing ahead of you if you want it.'

'You wouldn't mind a wife who works?'

'I want a wife who's happy,' Gordon told her with a swift kiss.

'I never really explained about Jack,'

Avril murmured.

'You don't have to. He's a scoundrel.' Gordon frowned.

'But I want to,' Avril persisted. 'I want you to know why I felt I was able to go away with him. I never, loved him, though.'

Gordon looked relieved. He pulled across two chairs for them to sit. Around them the party was starting up. Johnny's band had arrived and was tuning its instruments. Neighbours from the far end of the street appeared with more contributions of food. Children weaved in and out of the slower adults, shouting with glee and playing games.

'I craved excitement in my life and Jack offered that,' Avril admitted. 'But when I realised I loved you, I knew I had to tell him I couldn't see him any more. By then I didn't care even to keep him as a friend. The more I got to know him, the more I realised how different we were.'

'But then you saw Lucille's letters,'

Gordon prompted gently.

'Yes, and I was so hurt that I reacted blindly on impulse. Jack asked me to marry him and I agreed. To be honest, I was so angry I'd have run away anyway. Jack's offer was fortuitous, that's all.' Avril's fingers interlaced tightly as she continued, 'But he wasn't going to marry me. He lied. I was such a fool. I'd messed things up terribly but I knew I couldn't come home.'

'It was my fault,' Gordon interrupted, unable to witness Avril's distress. 'If I hadn't been so reticent, so afraid to take the chance on happiness, I would've told you I loved you and asked you to marry me right there and then. I was scared and I didn't feel I deserved a second chance at life. I was a fool.'

'We were fools together.' Avril laughed weakly. 'But we can put it behind us now, can't we?'

'Of course we can. I suggest we think no more on it, but try your mother's tasty chicken dish and pay our compliments to the chef,' Gordon said, deliberately lightly. He pulled Avril up from her chair, gave her a reassuring kiss and guided her to the trestles where Mrs Petrocelli stood, rather bewildered, having been left in charge of a large, shiny ladle.

Lucille arrived as Johnny's band began to play. Avril was surprised to see her. For some reason she'd imagined her safely far away, back up in the Highlands.

She managed a smile when Lucille came to say hello and ask in a subdued tone if she might have a private word with Gordon. Avril watched the two of them walk off along the street. She was secure. She knew Gordon belonged to her. But what did Lucille have to say?

'Isn't this brilliant?' Peggy cried, flinging herself into Gordon's vacant chair. 'When's the dancing going to start? That's what I want to know. Oh, Avril, it's good to have you back. It would've been horrid you living in London.'

Peggy was in fully party mode. She

was wearing a full blue pleated skirt with a red and white striped shirt, and crimson shoes complete with little bows. Her cropped blonde hair was glossy and her lips painted to match her shoes.

'It is brilliant,' Avril agreed. 'And I'm glad I'm here. I never want to leave again.'

'I'm surprised you let Gordon speak to that woman.' Peggy narrowed her eyes at the two distant figures in the noisy crowd.

Avril laughed. 'He's not under my thumb, Pegs. Besides, Lucille can do no more harm. I feel sorry for her if anything.'

'Hmm, well. He's a handsome man, your Gordon. You'll be fending off the girls.'

'Like you, you mean?' Avril teased.

Peggy blushed. 'I wouldn't dare. I admit I did have a fancy for him, but it was clear he had eyes only for you, even if you were the last to notice it, dear friend. Besides, there are plenty more fish in the sea,' she finished, glancing slyly along the street.

Avril followed her gaze, hoping it was leading to poor Davey. But no. Davey was strumming on his guitar, looking delighted to be a part of Johnny's band for the day. Peggy was looking in the opposite direction. There were older couples and scampering children and groups eating at picnic tables.

'Over there,' Peggy said helpfully. Avril looked again. A young, dark-haired man sat with an older couple, eating and chatting.

'That's Sean. He's an Australian, come visiting his relatives. He's just arrived and is staying for six months.' Peggy gave a very satisfied sigh.

'I hope he likes blondes,' Avril said, poking Peggy's ribs until she squealed. 'Let's get some food before it all vanishes.'

* * *

The water lapped gently at the riverbank. Without thinking, they'd

302

walked this way, music and laughter fading behind them.

'I didn't expect you to stay, Lucille,' Gordon said. 'I thought you'd be on your way home.'

'It's a holiday so no transport, but I wasn't ready to go in any case. I wanted to apologise to you properly.'

'There's no need.'

'Yes, there is. I've behaved very wrongly to you and you've been so good to me. You've been a brother and a friend. I see that now and, what's more, I see its true value. I've been in a bad place for a very long time, you know that, Gordon. But funnily, I can see a hope now for the future. You shocked me when you said you wouldn't see me ever. It made me realise I need to change.'

'I will always be there for you, Lucille,' Gordon promised. 'You are like my little sister. Avril and I will be your good friends.'

Lucille pulled a wry face. 'I don't think Avril will be my friend and I can't

303

say I blame her. I behaved appallingly to her.'

'You underestimate her,' Gordon countered. 'She has a loving heart. She'll warm to you, I guarantee it.'

They both stared out at the great river. The ships were blasting their horns in tribute to the new Queen. A flotilla of mallards bobbed merrily on the slow waves.

'So what will you do now?' Gordon asked her soberly.

Lucille kicked a pebble. It fell into the water and sank below rings of water.

'I'm going home first, to see my parents. I owe them that. Then I'm coming back here to the city. I want a fresh start.'

'Any plans?'

'Avril's brother, Davey, has been kind to me. He's talking of opening a music shop. I could see myself helping with that.'

They started on their return to the party, the sounds of the river now to their backs. Lucille laid her hand hesitantly on his arm. Gordon looked at her, waiting.

'I'm not forgetting him,' she said quietly. 'I still think about him every day, but I'm trying to move on. Ronnie would want that.' Her pale eyes sought his reassurance.

'Yes, Ronnie would want that,' Gordon agreed, and knew that it was true.

Davey waved to Lucille as they reached the party throng and Gordon knew she'd be fine.

* * *

Avril saw a face she wasn't expecting in the crowd. She pushed her way as politely as possible through the bodies until she got to a table of five.

'Hello, Agnes — I'm glad to see you.'

The young woman looked uncomfortable. Beside her, round the table, were Gloria, Shirley, Helen and a little girl who was clearly a smaller sister.

'Your mum invited Helen. She couldn't come on her own,' she muttered.

Avril noticed Agnes had made a real effort, even if she was just escorting her younger sister. Her hair was clasped in the same way as at the dance hall, and she had on make-up. Her navy polka dot dress was clean, even if there was a frayed edge to her sleeve. It was a dress which had been worn many times and cared for, to make do.

Like the soft fool she was, Avril's throat tightened. If only they could feed and befriend all the Agnes and Helens of the city. Perhaps her articles would help change conditions in some small way. She itched to write more.

Instead she reached for a chair and, without asking, joined the group. Agnes moved over awkwardly to let her in.

'Cake?' she asked shortly, pushing the plate towards Avril.

'Cake,' she agreed and although she didn't really want one, she took it. It wasn't a cake, it was the beginning of a dialogue. The silence was broken by Gloria's snort. She pointed at Helen.

'What?' the girl demanded.

Shirley giggled. 'You've got a blob of cream on the end of your nose.'

Then they were all giggling together, even Agnes, and the atmosphere mellowed.

As the sky darkened, the illuminations came on and the whole of Aline Street was lit up.

'It's so pretty,' Avril gasped.

'The neighbours have been busy,' Gordon agreed, watching with her. Couples were dancing now in the empty stretch of road. The older people sat at the tables, chatting and no doubt reminiscing on their own dancing days.

Lucille danced with Davey, who'd given up his guitar and place in the band so that he could partner her. Peggy, triumphant, was letting Australian Sean lead her in a dance that bore little resemblance to the real steps. It gave Peggy opportunities to bump into him teasingly and sashay away.

Sean was smitten. He'd danced with no one else except a determined Gloria who'd nabbed him earlier in the evening. Now Gloria danced with Helen, while Shirley had to make do with her father who was slow due to his disability. Mr Phillips had gallantly asked Mrs Petrocelli to dance and they moved around crab-like, ignoring the beat and reliving some of their own youth.

Gordon grabbed Avril, pulling her onto the street to dance.

'How's your leg?' she asked doubtfully.

'Tender after the driving,' he admitted. 'And not helped by scrambling down the canalside, but all in all, not too bad. Besides, we can't not dance on this night of all nights.'

'I wonder what we'll be like when we're old,' Avril murmured, as they passed the elderly lodgers moving slowly in circles.

'We'll still be very much in love, of course,' Gordon mused as he waltzed her round. 'Plus our six children and flocks of grandchildren will keep us entertained.'

'You want children?'

Gordon stopped mid-step. 'We never discussed it, but yes, I do. Why are you crying, Avril? Darling, what is it? If you don't want any, then that's okay too. It's you I want most of all.'

'I want children.' Avril wiped away her tears. 'I'm being silly. I'm crying because I'm so happy. What about living in a big white house with its own garden and an apple tree and a pond?'

'We could put a swing for the children on the apple tree and have a puppy to frolic in the pond.' Gordon chuckled.

'I love you,' Avril whispered.

'I love you, too.' Gordon sealed it with a kiss. Linda Garnett frowned disapprovingly from the other side of a trestle where she was still handing out plates.

'I've upset your Mum. Looks as if Plan A needs to be brought forward,'

Gordon said hastily, leaving Avril confused.

The band stopped playing and Gordon stood there. Everyone quietened and turned to see why there was no music.

'Good evening, everybody. I hope you're all having a great time.' Gordon gave a nervous cough. 'I won't interrupt the dancing for more than a minute but I have an announcement to make.' He allowed a dramatic pause. Linda was still frowning. David Garnett made his way towards her, knowing what was coming. He put his arm around his wife's shoulders as Gordon continued, 'I want you all to know that Miss Avril Garnett has done me the honour of agreeing to marry me.'

There was a brief moment of silence while the news sank in, then Peggy screamed and Davey whistled and the crowd burst into applause. Avril was surrounded by congratulations and warm hugs. Across everyone, she saw her parents smiling. Gordon was forgiven. Linda welcomed him to the family with an embrace. David winked. Gordon had formally asked him for Avril's hand in marriage before he drove off in the car to save her. He'd kept the secret well.

The music started up again in a lively waltz and David and Linda took to the floor. Gordon offered to dance with Shirley who was delighted. Avril noticed that Davey was still dancing with Lucille. She hoped he'd be happy with her.

As the party swirled around her, Avril found herself thinking about Jack. What had happened to him? Had the two men caught up with him — was Jack even alive? Even though he'd treated her so badly, Avril prayed for his safety. She hoped he was all right and had reached London. She'd told Gordon she never loved Jack and it was true, but there was a part of her that cared about him despite what had happened.

Her life could have taken a very different turn yesterday. She was grateful for the way it had turned out and that she was here. But where was Jack?

18

Western Australia, 1962.

Dear Avril

You will wonder why I'm writing to you now out of the blue, nine years after I had to leave you in circumstances that were not ideal. The answer is that this is not the first letter I've written you. I have tried and tried over the years to explain myself on paper. Each time I've torn it up, thrown it in the bin and decided not to try again.

But now I must do it. My life has taken a sudden and unexpected turn. It's time to close the door on my past. It's haunted me, you have to know that. That moment when you ran from me across the field and I was stuck. I could have followed you and pleaded with you to come with me. But Shorty and Gibbs were almost on me. I admit I was scared mainly for myself. But I led them away from you and I saved myself by running. I left you and as I did so I realised I loved you. I would have married you, if that was important to you. We could have had a life together. Even when I reached London and managed to elude them, I thought of coming back for you. I dreamed of you welcoming me with open arms. Of you agreeing to start again. But inside I knew it wouldn't happen like that. You loved the lodger chap, what's his name — I forget. What happened? Did you marry him? Did you have the children you wanted?

Anyway it's not important now. I like to think you cared for me a little. I want to believe you thought about me after I was gone.

So I'm writing to tell you I made it after all. It didn't work out living with my old man. So I took a chance and bought a ticket to Australia. You should see the place. It's vast, with miles to the horizon. Plenty of opportunities for guys like me. I set up a little business of this and that. I'm doing all right. I met a girl and settled down. And yesterday, at the grand old age of thirty-nine, I became a father. A girl. You know already what she's named.

I'll never forget you, Avril. I'm glad to have finished this letter. It's time it got sent. Think kindly on me when you read it. It was sent with the best of wishes

From your loving Jack.

19

So he had survived. How very like Jack Lafferty the letter was, Avril thought, shaking her head with wry amusement. He'd justified running off as a way of saving her when actually he was intent on saving his own skin! Mind you, if he'd stayed, what would the two men have done to him? It didn't bear imagining.

She was glad he was alive and had made a better life for himself. His declaration of love startled her. He would have married her after all!

It was good to know that he wasn't completely the black-hearted scoundrel he'd seemed at the time. There was a streak of goodness and of decency in Jack, struggling to get to the surface. It had always worried her over the years, that she could have been so duped by him. It had shaken her belief in herself and in her judgement of others' characters. He would have married her. That alternative life hung shadily in her mind.

But there was no comparison. Her feelings for Jack, whatever they had been, were pale wisps compared to the strong, heady relationship she'd shared and enjoyed down the years with Gordon. She'd made the right decisions and chosen the right man. Still . . . it was nice to think that a little Australian Avril existed on the far side of the world. It was a touching tribute from Jack. She wondered if he'd ever told his wife why he'd chosen the name.

The doorbell rang.

'It's all right, Mum. I'll get it,' the young Avril said. It was probably Mr Phillips who'd forgotten his keys as usual.

Gloria held onto her arm. 'Gran, it's okay. Uncle John's getting the door.'

Avril peered at her. Inge's concerned face loomed. 'Are you okay, Gran? Did you enjoy your letter?'

317

'My letter . . . ? Yes.' Avril clutched it. 'Where's Grandad?'

'Right here, darling.' Gordon's deep voice sounded behind her. He kissed the top of her head. 'Who's written to you?'

'It's Jack,' Avril said. 'You can read it if you like.' She offered up the thin piece of paper.

Gordon hesitated, then shook his head. 'I don't need to.'

John came back into the room, looking baffled but pleased. 'That was our neighbour, Barry. He and his wife Penny are holding a barbecue and asked if we'd all like to join them. There'll be other neighbours invited too.'

'Barry and Penny. Is that the young couple at number eight?' Lisa asked.

'He's got red hair and she's got glasses.' John quickly described them. 'What do you say?'

'It's a great idea. Looks like Mum'll get her Diamond Jubilee street party after all,' Graham joked. 'Right — everyone out!'

'I'll fix up some food to bring over,' Lisa called to John. She and Hildegard vanished into the kitchen happily discussing what they could take.

'Mum, are you okay to walk over?' John asked with concern.

'Of course I am,' Avril said spiritedly. 'I'm not quite in my dotage yet. Besides, Dad'll be with me.' She grabbed Gordon's arm for support and they headed out to the neighbours.

'Hello! Welcome,' Barry and Penny called. There was a large gas-fed barbecue in pride of place on the patio. Around it were picnic tables with paper plates and napkins and glasses ready and waiting. Other neighbours were arriving and introducing themselves. Barry threw burgers and sausages onto the barbecue while his wife poured drinks. Inge found a girl her own age to talk to while Lucy was soon running about with two small boys belonging to a tall lady from further up the street.

'Will there be dancing later?' Avril asked Gordon. 'Remember the fun we

319

had at the Coronation! What a night that was. We danced until our feet hurt. And you told everyone we were getting married. Mum and Dad were so overjoyed.'

'We could still give the youngsters a run for their money over the dancing,' Gordon said gamely.

'Peggy would love this,' Avril mused. 'She and Sean are coming over in the autumn, by the way.'

'Probably for a rest from all their grandchildren.' Gordon laughed. Peggy had married Australian Sean six months after they met at the Coronation street party and they'd moved to Australia. They'd produced five children and twenty grandchildren with a couple of great grandchildren on the way. They came back to the UK every other year so Avril and Peggy were able to catch up. Gordon and Avril had visited them, too, several times.

'I wonder how life would've turned out if Peggy had married Davey?' Avril mused.

'Peggy and Davey? What are you talking about, dear? That was never on the cards. Besides, Davey and Lucille are devoted to one another. It's what inspires their music.' Gordon put his arm round his wife. 'We've had a great life together, haven't we, love?'

Avril curled into his embrace. She fitted so well into that comforting and loving space. 'It's not over yet,' she declared. 'I fully intend to be around to see more great-grandchildren.'

Gordon took two plates of food from Inge who was in a helpful mood. 'And it's our own diamond wedding later this year, too. How do you want to celebrate that?'

Avril sat gratefully to eat the barbecue meat and salad. It was good to take the weight off her legs. She looked about at the party of people getting to know each other, brought together by the special celebration for the Queen.

Her own family were mingling and chatting, enjoying the social occasion.

John and Lisa were talking to Barry and Linda, and Avril was sure that a friendship was being forged which would blossom over the garden fence. Their son Alexander sat dandling baby Ross on his lap, engrossed by his baby son and his joyful gurgles. His wife Jennifer was watching their daughter Lucy play with the other kids, ready to step in when tempers frayed or knees got scraped. Graham was talking to Hildegard. They were rarely apart and enjoyed each other's company immensely, even now after so many years of marriage. Hopefully she and Gordon had set a good example with their own lifelong love affair.

Inge was circulating, making sure everyone had enough to eat and drink. Petra was standing shyly to one side, sipping her drink. In a moment Avril would go to her. But first she had to answer Gordon's question.

'I don't care where we go to celebrate our diamond wedding,' she said. 'All I want is all our family around us.' She was slightly tearful. A faint echo of her mother saying 'don't be soft' floated on the air.

'You miss Mark.' Gordon hugged her tight.

Avril sniffed. 'I wrote to him. I told him we were all getting together for the Jubilee. I had hoped . . . '

'He does have a busy job,' Gordon reminded her gently. 'Besides, your letter may not have reached him. He's supposed to get his mail sent on to him, but from Bolivia to Georgia is quite a trek for one small envelope.'

Avril pondered afresh the journey Jack's letter must have taken across the continents and ocean and the fullness of time to reach her. She hoped he'd had a good life in the fifty years separating his words on the paper and her reading of it. Little Avril would herself be fifty now, she realised with a jolt.

There was a bubble of noise at the entrance to the garden. Perhaps another neighbour arriving, guided by the smell of sizzling sausages and the sound of people having fun.

Avril settled back into the chair. She didn't need to go and talk to Petra now. Petra was being chatted to by a young fellow of about her own age with a thick shock of auburn hair. She was prettily flushed and kept flicking her long honey ponytail back over her shoulder. Avril smiled; the cogs and wheels kept going round. The young believed they had invented everything. They didn't think to look back, to peel back the layers of years.

Suddenly someone clapped large, warm hands over her eyes. 'Guess who?'

Avril's heart leapt. 'Mark! You made it! You came home!'

'Don't cry, Mum. You always do that.' Mark offered her his handkerchief, hunkering down beside his tiny, fragile mother.

He looked the picture of health, ruddy and tanned. She was struck by how much like her Dad he was. If she stuck him in an allotment and put a pipe in his hand, she'd be transported back to those happy days.

Gordon was there now, pleased with Mark and glad for Avril. The others crowded round to greet Mark. Gordon reached for her hand and they entwined their fingers. Together they sat surrounded by the loving circle of their family.

THE END

We do hope that you have enjoyed reading this large print book.

Did you know that all of our titles are available for purchase?

We publish a wide range of high quality large print books including:
Romances, Mysteries, Classics
General Fiction
Non Fiction and Westerns

Special interest titles available in large print are:
The Little Oxford Dictionary
Music Book, Song Book
Hymn Book, Service Book

Also available from us courtesy of Oxford University Press:
Young Readers' Dictionary
(large print edition)
Young Readers' Thesaurus
(large print edition)

For further information or a free brochure, please contact us at:
Ulverscroft Large Print Books Ltd.,
The Green, Bradgate Road, Anstey,
Leicester, LE7 7FU, England.
Tel: (00 44) **0116 236 4325**
Fax: (00 44) **0116 234 0205**

DESTINY CALLING

Chrissie Loveday

It is 1952. William Cobridge has returned from a trip to America a different man. Used to a life of luxury, he had been sent away to learn about life in the real world. He meets teacher Paula Frost on a visit to see her aunt, the housekeeper at Cobridge House. He is keen to see Paula again and asks her for a date. Could this be the start of a new romance? But then, things never go smoothly . . .

WHERE I BELONG

Helen Taylor

When a mysterious Italian man arrives on the doorstep in a storm, Maria can hardly turn him away, even though the guesthouse is closed for the winter. Maria's gentle care helps Dino recover from his distressing news, and soon she risks losing her heart to this charismatic stranger. But he has commitments that will take him far away, and her future is at the guesthouse. Can two people from different walks of life find a way to be together?

WED FOR A WAGER

Fenella Miller

Grace Hadley must enter into a marriage of convenience with handsome young Rupert Shalford, otherwise Sir John, her step-father, will sell her to the highest bidder. But Rupert's older brother Lord Ralph Shalford has other ideas and is determined he will have the union dissolved. However, Sir John is equally determined to recover his now missing step-daughter. Will Grace ever find the happiness she deserves?

OUR DAY WILL COME

Sally Quilford

When handsome American airman Ben Greenwood walks into the Quiet Woman pub, the landlord's pretty daughter Betty Yeardley is immediately attracted to him. But Betty is promised to Eddie Simpson, who has been missing in action for two years. With a stocking thief putting the villagers of Midchester on edge, and Eddie's parents putting pressure on Betty to keep her promise, she is forced to fight her growing feelings for Ben.